STORIES FROM THE LAND OF JEWELS

LOVE & LIFE

LOVE STORIES FROM MANIPUR

BY

SOPHIA CHANU

ACKNOWLEDGMENTS

I am profoundly grateful to my parents for the life they have given me. Their love, guidance, and sacrifices have shaped me into the person I am today.

My heartfelt thanks go to my dear friend, Di Raj, for designing my cover and offering unwavering support throughout this author journey. Her invaluable insights, keen observation and attention to detail have been very helpful at every stage of my journey.

A special thanks to Sir Som Bathla, Amazon Bestselling Author and Entrepreneur, and his Author Freedom Hub, for his mentorship, motivation, and guidance in writing, self-publishing, and launching books on Amazon.

I extend my gratitude to Sir Ravi Tewari for his guidance, motivation, and support at every stage of the process. His insights and encouragement have been instrumental in bringing this project to fruition. I also appreciate his team's efforts in designing and formatting the book, making it ready for publication.

Last but not the least, I also thank my three younger sisters for their love, support and encouragement.

Thank you all for being a part of this incredible journey of writing and publishing this book.

Thank you, my dear readers, for choosing to embark on this adventure with me. Your support and encouragement mean a lot to me.

DEDICATION

To my dear readers!

This book is for you. Thank you for opening these pages and embarking on this journey with me. Your support and enthusiasm will make every word worthwhile.

About this Novel

The stories in this book encompass the vast spectrum of emotions - from the warmth of love to the sting of unlove, from joy to pain.

I have penned these stories with respect and sensitivity, aiming not to hurt, but to shed light on the intricate human experiences we all share.

I humbly request you to bear with me through the dreams, the hope, the hurt, the disappointment, the pain, and the complexities of love and life portrayed within these pages.

It is my hope that you will find reflection, empathy, and perhaps a sense of solidarity as you read these stories.

Thank you for your understanding and for joining me in this exploration of the multifaceted nature of love and life.

Contents

1

Love Unfolded

Tender love bloomed
From laughter shared,
Gently nurtured with care,
Through time and trial.

In a small town in Bihar, as the setting sun casts its reddish orange hue in the sky, Sanjay and Gita sat on their veranda, sipping their evening tea. The silence hung between them like a thick cloud, heavy and laden with concern for their son. This is the kind of concern that only parents of a single marriageable son could understand.

"Rishi's Papa, it's been three years since Rishi left for Germany," Gita's voice broke the silence, her tone laced with worry. "He's doing well as a software engineer, but..."

"But he's alone, Gita. He needs a partner, someone to share his life with," Sanjay replied, his gaze lost in the distance.

Gita nodded, her hands fidgeting with the edge of her saree. "I know, but he dismisses the idea whenever we discuss

marriage. The girls are never right for him. Too this, too that...
What does he want?"

Sanjay shook his head, "He seems to be waiting for
someone, and he doesn't even know who she is..."

Gita signed, "How long should he wait? All his friends have
gotten married; he is way past marriageable age...I am so
worried."

Sanjay soothed his wife, "Don't worry, I am sure he will find
someone soon."

As the night crept in, they talked about Rishi, their son,
miles away in Germany, living a life they were proud of but
knew little about. They reminisced about his childhood, his
achievements, and his stubborn refusal to settle down.

Meanwhile, Rishi sat before his computer in Germany, eyes
staring blankly at his screen filled with lines of code. His mind
wasn't on his work; it was on his last Skype call with his
parents. Their hopeful faces, their veiled disappointment.
They wanted him to settle down; he knew that, but he couldn't
accept just anyone.

"I want someone who understands me, and can answer the
questions in my heart, someone I will instantly recognise as
my other half.... Someone who can understand my dreams and
will share hers with me," he muttered.

♥

In the quiet solitude of his room, the computer screen's soft glow illuminated his face as he worked tirelessly into the night. The world outside was asleep, but his mind was alive with thoughts and tasks. During his late-night session, a flicker on his screen caught his attention—a glitch that seemed to beckon him towards a forgotten digital folder.

As the images materialised before his eyes, a wave of nostalgia washed over him. There they were, his classmates, his closest friends through the years from VTU to IIM, Bangalore, frozen in time: Nita with her infectious laughter, Rahul with his ever-present book, Kanchan with her thoughtful gaze, Ravi with his mischievous grin, and then, there was Roma, right in the centre, a vision of grace with her dreams shining in her eyes. Her slender figure was poised with elegance, her eyes sparkled with a vivacity that outshone the stars, and her smile, oh, that smile, it warmed him up like a ray of sunshine as he gazed at that smile. Her black hair cascaded down her shoulders in soft waves. He found himself wondering, "Was she always this beautiful? This radiant? How had I never seen it?"

Memories of the day they had met for the first time came to life in his mind.

The sun-drenched streets of Bangalore hummed with the energy of the bustling city, where students from across India converged to pursue their dreams. He had come to Bihar to fulfil his dreams. He was intelligent and very ambitious. His sharp intellect and unwavering determination had earned him a coveted spot in the prestigious engineering college VTU, Bangalore.

It was the day that he had come for enrollment in his engineering course. He was paying fees at the counter. A soft voice called out to him, "Excuse me, you are standing on my dupatta" he looked down and saw that he had indeed stepped on the dupatta of a gorgeous damsel with shining bright eyes who glared at him. "I am so sorry, it's the queue; it's so crowded that I didn't realise," he mumbled, stepping away from her piece of clothing and apologising profusely for his mistake.

She was in the lady's queue right next to him. He finished first, then hung around for some time, watching her complete paying her fees.

"Excuse me," he said as she was moving away after her work was done. "I am so sorry that I was completely dumb and didn't even notice when I was stepping on your clothes...... Can I help you in any way?"

She smiled and replied, "No thanks, bye". He watched her walk away with the jet-black curls cascading down her back. He had never seen anyone so beautiful in his life; she looked like a princess from a fairy tale.

He was overjoyed when he realised that she was in the same class as he was. Amid the challenging and sometimes daunting lectures delivered by the stalwart Professors of the reputed institution, he often caught himself quietly staring at her as she radiated brilliance and intelligence in class. She was always found with her two close friends, Nita and Kanchan, who were inseparable. She was thus unapproachable until Nita and Kanchan became friends with his two close friends, Ravi and Rahul. Then, the six of them started hanging out together.

Memories of their shared experiences assailed his senses. They explored Bangalore's busy streets, lanes, and bylanes every Sunday. The malls became their playgrounds, the cinemas their escape. Together with their friends, they explored all the secrets of the town, the tourist spots, the amusement parks, and the botanical gardens, and they also tasted the varied cuisine of its restaurants.

After weekday classes, the campus library was their sanctuary, not just as a place for studies but a place where they shared whispered consultations and made plans about their next outing. Their discussions were as varied as the books that lined the shelves.

Time passed slowly with the rhythm of classes, the intensity of studies, the pressure of exams, and the swift passage of years. They believed they might never meet again after VTU Bangalore, but it was as if fate conspired to reunite the friends again within the esteemed halls of IIM Bangalore. There, their bond flourished anew as they shared Sundays filled with camaraderie, crammed for exams amidst the hushed tones of the library, and revelled in the joy and laughter of their shared outings. Their friendship remained steadfast through the seasons of academic rigour and became an enduring connection until they triumphantly completed their management courses at IIM Bangalore.

After Rishi graduated from IIM, he got a job at a reputed firm in Frankfurt, Germany, while Roma stayed in Bangalore. Rishi's younger sister Pinky and Roma worked in the same office, with Roma in a senior position. Roma's elder sister, Rita, also worked in Bangalore.

After so many years, he was seeing her with new eyes. He remembered how he had felt when he first saw her, feelings that he had crushed aside as they became good friends, and the pressures of their studies had made it necessary to snuff out whatever romantic feelings sparked in his heart.

His heart skipped a beat as he entertained the possibilities that now danced in his mind. He had harboured feelings for her, gentle like the first rays of dawn, yet he had never acknowledged his feelings even to himself, never dared to step out of the shadows.

Now, as he gazed upon Roma's image, he realised that amidst the camaraderie of their joint friendship with the others, he had missed seeing her as a lovable, enticing woman. It was as if a veil had been lifted, and he saw her for the first time—not just as a friend, but as something much more....

"Roma," he whispered to the stillness, " Were you always this beautiful? No .... I knew you were beautiful. It's just that I never allowed myself to feel this way..."

The silence of the night bore witness to his restlessness; the only sounds were the soft hum of the computer and the distant call of the night. But in his heart, a decision was forming, a resolve to no longer ignore the new stirrings of his heart.

In Imphal, a place graced with pleasant weather all year round, where the air carried the scent of jasmine and the monsoon rains carpeted the ground in lush green, Roma's mother, Tampakleima, fretted. Her daughter, Roma, was a rare gem—a brilliant student who was as beautiful as she was intelligent. But she was growing older, and the suitors who came knocking were like fleeting fireflies—bright for a moment, then gone. She rejected them outright after the first meeting, too. It seemed as if the man who would marry her was nowhere to be found in their beautiful State of Manipur.

Her husband, Manisana, had passed away a few years back. Her son, Sanamani, Roma's elder brother, was already married and had two young kids —a young son, Sanatomba and a daughter, Rabina — and now it was time for Roma to settle down.

Meanwhile, in the bright and busy city of Bangalore, Roma sat by her window, her fingers tracing the raindrops on the glass. She knew her parents' concern and felt it like a weight on her shoulders. But Roma was different. While other girls her age giggled over crushes and whispered secrets about boys, she immersed herself in books and enjoyed the quiet magic of solitude.

As the sky blushed twilight one evening, a time before the chaos of the day gave way to the stillness of the night, Roma lit a diya in her small puja corner. The flickering flame danced, casting shadows on the idols of gods and goddesses. She closed her eyes and whispered her heart's longing to the deity she revered—the fierce and enigmatic Goddess Kamakhya.

"Devi Maa[i]," Roma murmured, "grant me a life partner who understands the language of my soul. Someone who will walk beside me, not ahead or behind. A love that will bloom like the lotus in your sacred pond."

The monsoon winds carried her prayer beyond the city, across hills and rivers, until it reached the ancient temple of Goddess Kamakhya in Assam. There, perhaps She listened, Goddess Kamakhya. She understood Roma's quiet desires and her intense need to find the right person to walk proudly beside her and not stifle her with his self-centeredness.

Days turned into weeks, and Roma continued her daily rituals. She offered marigolds and incense, hoping her plea would reach the heavens. And then, one night, as the rain tapped insistently on her window, Roma dreamt.

In her dream, she stood at the edge of a lotus-filled pond. The water shimmered in the moonlight, and there, amidst the lotus flowers, stood a man. A man she knew.... a man who was always a good friend, but perhaps more than a good friend. A man she had never thought of as more than a friend but who had always been ready to help her in every way he could. He whispered to her: "Roma, I am your promise. I am the one who will understand your silence, celebrate your brilliance, and hold your hand through life's storms."

She called out his name, " Rishi", and woke up suddenly.

"Oh God, what a dream, but why did I dream of Rishi? He must already have gotten married by now", she wondered.

The office hummed with fluorescent lights and the soft murmur of keyboards. Her heart fluttered like a startled bird as Roma stepped through the glass doors. Today was different—spreadsheets or deadlines did not consume her thoughts. They travelled to the person closely linked to the man she had seen in her dream. Anticipation throbbed in her heart as she headed to a cubicle in the office, far away from her own.

Pinky. The name echoed in Roma's mind like a soft whisper. Pinky, Rishi's sister. She must talk to her and ask her how Rishi is.

As if summoned by fate, Pinky appeared at the end of the corridor. Her cheeks flushed; her eyes wide. "Didi Roma," she blurted out, "I was coming to meet you."

Roma's pulse quickened. "Why, what is it, Pinky?"

Pinky smiled coyly and said, "Didi, Can I please come to your place tonight? I have a surprise for you."

"What surprise is it, Pinky?" Roma was very curious, but Pinky only smiled mischievously and said, "It's a surprise, Didi", and returned to her office cubicle.

Roma's heart thudded painfully. After the dream she had, she was suddenly terrified.

Roma returned to her cubicle, but the dream nagged at her. She worked hard to make sense of the figures that popped up on her laptop. Yet her thoughts swirled with questions. Anticipation built up to a crescendo in her heart; she felt restless.

The clock seemed to crawl, and she couldn't wait for 5 pm, the hour that promised answers. The time seemed to go softly, the clock ticking too slowly for her. She could not wait for the surprise ahead of her! The day stretched on, each tick of the clock a reminder of what might await her...

Finally, it was time for her to go home. Once she reached home, she tidied up the room, expecting Pinky to drop in any minute. After she indulged in a luxurious bath, let her hair down, and dressed in simple but elegant clothing, she sat in her drawing room, expectant. But she did not know what for. The door rang at precisely 6 pm. Her steps faltered as she went over to open the door. The moment she opened the door, he stood at her door with a bouquet of fresh flowers. Rishi. Pinky stood smiling beside him.

It was a dream, a storm of emotions. The man who had been her confidant, her laughter partner, her movie companion, her study mate—now, he stood before her, a familiar stranger. His smile ignited her soul, and the light in his eyes stole her breath.

He smiled, and she felt it tug at her heartstrings—a magnetic pull that bridged the years apart.

Pinky broke the silence, "Brother Rishi came yesterday; he told me you were classmates from long ago. He asked me to take you to your place. "

Roma beckoned them to come in. They sat and chatted. "Can you believe it's been five years?" Rishi asked.

"Five years, three months, and two days," she replied smiling, "but who's counting?"

They laughed, and their laughter filled the space between them like a shared melody, both familiar and new.

The years had been kind, etching their experiences into their faces, yet their eyes still sparkled with the youthful exuberance of their college days.

They shared their phone numbers; they talked about their careers. Over tea and snacks, they relived their past escapades. All too soon, it was time for the siblings to leave. Rishi promised to ring her and visit again.

As soon as he reached Frankfurt, Rishi rang. They connected on Facebook, Instagram and WhatsApp. Coordinating their time zones was often challenging. When it was 11 am in Frankfurt, it was already 2:30 pm in Bangalore. Rishi usually called Roma between 7 pm and 11 pm Frankfurt time, which coincided with Roma's busy office hours from 10:30 am to 2:30 pm in Bangalore, as Frankfurt is 3 hours and 30 minutes behind Bangalore.

When it was 9 pm for him, and he wished to hear her voice, she was busy at work. When she woke up, he was deep in slumber. Likewise, when he woke up, she was getting ready for work. Somehow, they managed to chat on WhatsApp at all odd hours of the day, replying sometimes minutes or hours late to each other's messages.

As friends, in real life, they had never chatted so intimately. On chats, they started sharing their experiences and their deepest secrets. Their bond strengthened over their phone calls and chats.

One day, over the phone, Rishi asked tentatively,

"Can I ask you an intimate question?". He was almost afraid she would reply with a firm no, but she meekly replied, "What is it? Ask away."

"Is there anyone in your life, Ahem...I mean, do you have a boyfriend?" Rishi asked, with a hint of nervousness in his voice. The Roma he knew would have glared at him − if she were standing in front of him − if he dared ask such questions, but the new Roma replied softly, "No, there is no one..."

"You know, I always looked forward to our Sundays, where we had so much fun together," he confessed, "I always wished that the others were not around and that we could have gone together, just the two of us".

"Oh... but it didn't look like it..." she answered softly.

"You always brought your two friends with you.... You seemed so pure, so aloof, so... out of reach. So, I forced myself to think of you as a friend... but today...I know it's more than that...."

Roma could not say anything...She drew in her breath sharply as a warm glow spread through her heart at his words.... She remembered how he had always been willing to help her if she ever needed anything...he had always been there for her...more than the others, and she had not even realised what he had meant to her...

Rishi continued, "I hope you feel the same."

Roma couldn't answer as an unfamiliar feeling coursed through her heart, and she felt she would burst from the sheer joy she felt at his words.

"Roma, are you there?"

"Yes", she could only whisper.

"Please tell me that you feel something", Rishi insisted.

"Why else would I be messaging you at all odd hours?" Roma spoke up and blushed crimson, though thankfully, he couldn't see it.

"I am coming to Bangalore soon", he promised.

He came. They chatted again over a cup of coffee. The quaint café buzzed with the gentle hum of conversation and the clinking of cups. They sat at a cosy corner table, a steaming pot of coffee and an assortment of snacks between them, remnants of their shared past laid out before them for them to pick and choose for endless reminiscence.

They made polite conversation. They chatted for what seemed like hours.

Finally, Rishi mustered up courage. He took a deep breath, the words he had rehearsed countless times now perched on the edge of his tongue. "Roma, I now know how much I loved you....and still love you. I don't want to have any regrets. I don't want to let another day go without telling you how much you mean to me.......... I hope you will find it in your heart to love me." He rambled on, stumbling over his own words.

The café seemed to fall silent around them, the world holding its breath as he slid a small, velvet box across the table towards her.

"I know it's too soon for you, but I hope what I feel for you will find its echo in your heart...Will you make me the happiest man alive? Will you marry me? Please say yes..." he pleaded, his voice barely above a whisper.

Her heart skipped a beat, the moment suspended in time. Then, with a joyous lilt, she said, "Yes....!"

Yes, he was the missing piece she hadn't known she needed. It felt as if lightning struck, igniting all past memories and awakening fresh new emotions. No words were needed. Both knew that they were meant to be one.

It was a match made in heaven, a tale of love that had shimmered patiently waiting to be told.

The next day, he rang up home. He couldn't wait to ring up his parents.

"Mom, you had been searching for a girl for me; I know who it must be. She was my classmate through the years from VTU to IIM, Bangalore. Her name is Roma, and she is from Imphal, Manipur. She is working in the same institute as Pinky in Bangalore now. "

Rishi's voice was filled with a hopeful excitement that seemed to travel across the telephone lines.

His mother's hesitant yet curious voice crackled through the phone, "Rishi, are you sure she is from a good family? We don't know anything much about Manipur."

"Do not worry, Mom. As I said, she works in a reputed institution and is even Pinky's senior in the office. Her family is also of royal lineage in Manipur. And I repeat, Mom, I do not want any other woman if you want me to get married..." Rishi's words were firm, leaving no room for doubt about his resolve.

Rishi's parents, Sanjay and Gita, hailing from the conservative town of Hajipur in Bihar, had already been searching for a suitable bride for almost a year now, one who would fit seamlessly into their family's customs and traditions. They were worried that a Manipuri girl might find it hard to adapt to their culture and tradition. They were wary of such kind of intercultural interracial marriages.

But Rishi was adamant. His heart was set, and they were helpless to change it.

Rishi returned to Germany, leaving behind a trail of bittersweet memories. Roma, with her heart straddling continents, continued her life in Bangalore. As the summer progressed, vacation time came – a time for rest and joyful reunion with her family.

Every day, Rishi rang, his voice bridging the distance, a constant reminder of a future they could have. "Roma, have you spoken to your family about us?" he would ask, a tinge of hope colouring his tone.

Hesitant yet hopeful, Roma turned to her mother, Tampakleima, the head of their small family since her father, Manisana, had passed away. "Ima[ii] , there's something I need to tell you ..." she began.

As Roma told her the story of Rishi and his proposal, her mother listened, her face etched with lines of worry, "Roma, my child, this is a big step. How will we ensure your safety so far from home?"

Her brother, Sanamani, echoed their mother's worries. "Roma, you know we only want what's best for you. But if you move to Germany, the distance... we will be so worried for you, and we can't meet as often as we would like to."

The conversations were long and laden with emotion, the family's love for Roma clashing with the fear of the unknown.

The sisters of Roma (Rita) and Rishi (Pinky) got together and persuaded both parents to agree to the bond. With gentle persuasion and heartfelt pleas, they convinced their parents to bless the union of Roma and Rishi.

It was in July, the rainy season, when the weather was not so hot anymore but raining heavily at times, Rishi's family embarked on a hopeful journey to Manipur, the Land of Jewels. Sanjay, her father, and Vijay, her brother, arrived in Imphal in high spirits. They were eager to meet Roma and her family. They liked Roma instantly; she was beautiful, graceful, and elegant, like a princess. They met Roma's family: her mother, Tampakleima, brother Sanamani, sister-in-law Nivedita and their two little kids, Sanatomba and Rabina.

When Roma's family voiced their worries about letting her daughter leave for a foreign country so far away from home, Sanjay soothed her,

"We understand your concerns," Sanjay spoke, with a sincere resonance in his voice, "but rest assured, Roma will be cherished and protected as our daughter."

The meeting of the families was a joyous event; they liked each other instantly. Gifts were given, each a symbol of love and commitment—fine clothes vibrant and adorned with tiny stars that twinkled like the real stars in the sky and jewellery that sparkled like the morning dew.

And then, amidst the laughter and the sharing of stories, the roka[iii] engagement ceremony was performed.

On an evening in November, when the weather was settling into the crisp air of Autumn and the leaves on trees and plants had turned a golden hue, the sacred union of Rishi and Roma was celebrated with the enchanting traditions of Manipur. The venue was Hotel Imphal, a vibrant Hotel in Manipur, which can be hired for such occasions. The Hotel was situated amidst the lush greenery of Imphal, and it was decorated lavishly for the occasion.

The Heijingpot – a pre-wedding ceremony where the two groups of people met and exchanged gifts, etc. was celebrated one day before the wedding day, and on the next day, the wedding festivities were in full swing. The bride, Roma, was adorned in the traditional potloi[iv] and radiant in her beauty. The groom, Rishi, came with his entourage and sat in the well-decorated pavilion, resplendent in his dhoti and kurta. The traditional music, the dances, and the ritual splendour showcased the tradition of the Meiteis of Manipur to the groom and his family.

Later, at an appropriate timing in the rituals, the groom sat in the centre of the courtyard, and the bride took her seven rounds around him, sprinkling him with flowers at the end of each round. At the end of the seven rounds, she was seated beside him; the couple exchanged garlands—threaded by the bride herself on the day of the Heijingpot— that celebrated their union.

The families and their friends and relatives showered them with blessings, it was as if the heavens rejoiced in the union of the two people in the holy bond of matrimony.

The marriage ceremony concluded, but the wedding celebration transcended borders as a grand reception was held at the groom's birthplace in Bihar.

Lights and colours lit up the reception hall. Screens placed strategically in the hall brought the Manipuri wedding celebration to life again. Guests were thus able to commemorate the joyous occasion that had unfolded previously in Imphal.

Laughter and music echoed through the halls as the guests revelled in the festivities. The couple, now united and resplendent in their finery, welcomed the guests. It was indeed a fairy tale come to life, a story of love that the people who witnessed the occasion would tell far and wide.

After the reception, the pair went on a short honeymoon to Kashmir. After a few days of bliss and togetherness, he returned to Germany, and she went to her job in Bangalore. Their hearts remain tethered by love and longing during their time apart. They missed each other terribly, counting down until the next reunion when destiny would again weave their paths together.

♥

As the dutiful wife, Roma visited her in-laws in Bihar, staying with them after the honeymoon ended.

For some weeks, the two were separated, their hearts aching.

Rishi rang every day, his calls bridging the distance between them. In Bangalore, Roma worked to complete all pending tasks, waiting patiently for her fiancé to return.

The anticipation of their reunion was both sweet and torturous.

And then, finally, he arrived with her visa in hand. Her heart leapt to her throat when their eyes met. The world narrowed to just the two of them.

His heart full of love, Rishi whispered, " Love, I have missed you so much – now nothing will part us, ever!

Roma replied, "Yes!" Echoing his sentiments. Their promise was sealed – a love that had weathered separation and was now unbreakable.

== Endnotes ==

(i) Mother in Hindi

(ii) Mother in Meiteilon(Language of the Meiteis), Meiteis being on - nowe of the major ethnic group in Manipur.

(iii) The Roka ceremony is a pre-wedding ritual in Indian wedding traditions that marks the union of the bride and groom's families and friends.

(iv) The bride's wedding dress.

2

The Abyss Between Us

Two hearts tried the game of love,

Their feelings undefined, words unspoken,

Incompatibility became a strident sound,

Ending what could have been.

A chasm formed that love could not bridge.

The words danced before his eyes—the world seemed to fall away beneath him. He fell like a house of cards, collapsing without life or volition. His face contorted as if pulled in different directions by unseen forces. The letter dropped from his grasp as though it burned him. The wind caught it, lifting it gently out through the open window...

The words had burned like a bright red flame, scorching his vision...

Dear Jiten,

I am deeply sorry for the pain this letter will cause you. The guilt of this moment is something I fear I may never overcome. But it must be done. It is wrong to continue when we are so ill-suited for each other. It simply cannot work.

I hope that one day, you will find it in your heart to forgive me... perhaps when you meet someone who will cherish you for who you are... in a way I never could.

With regret,

Sunita.

The cold floor became his refuge that night. He sat in stark silence as the wintry night progressed, its icy tendrils clutching at him. He was numb to the piercing chill, to the passage of time. His mind was a battlefield, with demons clashing, goading him with their sharp barbs.

One was urging him to go to her, to plead with her to give their relationship one last chance. Another prodded him to go and force her to change her mind, to whisk her away somewhere, as his forefathers had once done[i] . Take her by force, claim her as his own, and display the raw depths of his unrequited feelings. Yet another taunted him, telling him to go away from her forever, far away. To lose himself in the vast expanse of space. To become a wisp of nothingness. To forget her, for she was not worth the torment.

Memories of another day flashed across his mind's eye.

They were strolling along Uripok Kangchup Road with no particular destination in mind. She had suggested the long walk to talk. The sun blazed down, enveloping them with heat like molten lava. She had an umbrella, but she wasn't sharing it with him. He was used to the heat. City-bred people always find it harder to bear heat and discomfort. But he couldn't help wishing – that she would share the umbrella with him – he could then get closer to her and feel her overwhelming fragrance.

Vehicles blared at them, warning them to stay away as they streaked past as if running away from the heat. It was a busy stretch. But soon, they had reached the isolated part of the road.

She turned to him, her eyes blazed with intensity as she spoke, "I feel we are incompatible. Our relationship would never work!"

A cloud passed over his dark and handsome face. But he kept mum.

"Why won't you say anything?" she implored.

She craned her neck, trying to look directly into his eyes. He was tall, while she was short and petite.

"It's because you overwhelm me," he confessed, his voice barely above a whisper. He couldn't breathe at times, feeling her sheer presence. She did that to him. He was the one blushing deep red whenever she cast even a fleeting glance his way.

"That's precisely the problem," she countered. "Why do you allow me to overwhelm you? Treat me as an equal, a friend, not some object or deity." She looked down sadly with these words.

"How can that be? As it is, you have always been thrusting your qualifications down my throat." He retorted.

"That's not fair!" Her voice rose an octave higher as she spoke.

Even as he spoke, he recognised the injustice in his words. She had never boasted about her academic prowess. But the fact was there, pulsating between them with vibrant life, making him feel inadequate. The undeniable reality of their differing backgrounds stood as a wall separating them. She was city-born-and- bred, while he was coming to the bright lights from an obscure place. They were young. The world was their oyster. They could unravel its secrets together, gently. They had all the time in their lives. Yet, he had found it increasingly difficult to bridge the chasm between them.

"If we truly love each other, our differences shouldn't matter," she mused, "We need mental communion and understanding. Similar sociological backgrounds, personality differences, that's the ideal conditions for relationships to work...that's what I read, I think, if I remember correctly," She glanced sideways at him while an unexpected deep red stain suffused her cheeks. Fascinated, he stared at her...while she seemed to cringe inwardly...

"Oh! You don't even try to listen", she accused softly. "What I mean is... we need to connect. There should be no looking down or looking up between us. If we could share what's inside us...then everything would be fine". She went on in her shy, timid voice—that voice which always shook him to the depths.

"If you keep complaining, how will that help?" he retorted.

"I have to! Your silence unnerves me...especially when we are with my friends. They tease me about your shyness and complete silence in my presence. We can't communicate this way. Have you ever tried to find out what is inside this shell?" Here, she pointed a tiny finger at herself as if for emphasis.

"Understanding takes time... we hardly know each other. I'm never at ease with you. My feelings are overwhelming—I love you too much..." He sounded pathetic, even to himself, but somehow, the words gushed out from his mouth like an over-flooded stream; he couldn't dam the flood.

His words silenced her. Did he sense her squirm with discomfort, or was it just his overactive imagination? Or did she give a shy, pleased smile, the corners of her soft mouth turned up slightly in triumph? He will never be sure.

How had they ever drifted into a relationship? Had she ever loved him? It must have been just a 'physical attraction' in the beginning. They had never really communicated, except to steal shy glances at each other whenever they met on the university lawns where she was pursuing her MA in Biochemistry, and he was studying English literature.

She and her friend, Mina, were always smiling, shy, and awkward when they passed them, along with his friend Ratan. When she walked by, an invisible current seemed to flow from her to him, electrifying his senses. And when their eyes met, he felt the fire in them, and his heart smouldered.

♥

After months of hanging around, waiting to glimpse her sweet face, he decided to do something. He finally confided in Ratan, which wasn't so tricky, as Ratan already knew. So, one day, while they were waiting at a bus stop, Ratan walked up to Mina, introduced themselves, and used the excuse of a non-existent sister who needed help with some guidance on what books to study for the upcoming Biochemistry entrance test. That was that...

From that day onwards, they went home, waited for the bus, and got down at the same stop. From there, he walked her to Thong Nambonbi[ii] , where she took a rickshaw home. Initially, both tried to prolong the walk from the bazaar to the bridge, but...

They couldn't open up to each other. They only conversed about the weather, the bad roads, and other mundane things. Sometimes, he couldn't even speak in her overwhelming presence. But he wrote and gave her his heart in written words. She responded with passionate letters of her own. Initially, she poured out her feelings on paper — how she had always been attracted to him and always waited for him to come into her life. She must have led a very lonely life. Her brilliance and her shyness were her prison walls. Most men felt inferior to her, and her shyness, which kept her quiet always, was seen as pride and ego. At least, that was what she told him in her letters.

Ever since they became a "pair," things began to change unpredictably. For him, her physical presence was intoxicating—the way she moved, her tiny gestures, her shy smile, the husky timbre of her voice. He was entangled, overwhelmed. Hence his inability to speak in her presence. Instead, with his face flushed red, he would struggle to control his feelings. Seeing his complete confusion in her presence, she grew more distant, withdrawing more and more from him. He began to notice the gulf stretching between them. Six months...and they were getting nowhere.

He longed to crush the agony and scatter it like wind-blown dust. He wanted to hold her, to soothe her doubts away. But she impaled him with sharp thorns of discontent. His sense of inadequacy seemed to exacerbate the problem, even though she always maintained that his lack of understanding about her had irritated her. What lurked within her obscure depths? She was an enigma, a mystery to him. He lacked the key to unravel the profound secrets of her heart. Perhaps therein lay his weakness and mistake.

He remembered the day it all ended....

They sat together in one of the city's restaurants, tucked away in a quiet, cosy corner. Other couples smiled, cooed, and gazed deeply into each other's eyes. However, they were like two strangers facing a vast chasm between them, seemingly intending to, yet unable to find a welcoming bridge.

"Jiten, tell me about yourself—your family," she said, looking quite enticing with her dark, smouldering eyes.

He managed to utter a few words. He wanted to share everything —his simple, happy family—a family filled with comfort, warmth, and affection. But words failed him, and silence settled between them. She watched him fumble with the trappings of eating in a big city restaurant, her pity evident. How could he ever handle his inadequacy and maintain calm and pose?

"Why don't you ask about me? Don't you want to know?" Her anger flared. She brushed away with her small, dainty hands a stray wisp of hair that kept falling across her eyes. He longed to tuck that wisp of hair away from her face and touch her. Fascinated by her every movement, the childlike expressions flitting across her sweet face, he stared.

"Stop staring at me like that!" her expressive face indicated annoyance as she snapped rudely at him.

"I am sorry....do tell me about your family". He snapped out of his trance.

"You are not interested in me- not in my mind. It's just my outer shell that you want". She hissed at him.

"Why do you say that? You imagine too much". He protested lamely. But she was resolute.

"Yes. I have been blind. This is not love, Jiten. I have always searched for love. I know how it should be. This is not the real thing."

She was getting up from her seat.

"Yes, you are not interested in my mind at all. We should part ways before it goes further."

She stormed out of the restaurant before he could stop her. He hurriedly paid the bill and followed, but she had already hailed a rickshaw. He was left standing alone, a big hollow within him.

They were mentally miles apart, a realisation that dawned on him now. The chasm between them was insurmountable. He had never indeed known her. What did she genuinely desire from life? Contrary to his assumptions, she had always maintained that she wasn't materialistic. All she sought was love, true love. But what did true love mean to her? Hadn't he loved her sincerely? Or had he truly loved her at all? Could one love something about which they knew nothing? Was she merely a beautiful flower he yearned to crush in his hands?

He never attempted to reach out to her. After her farewell letter, he wrote one last letter wishing her a life filled with happiness and the fulfilment of all her desires. He didn't plead for another chance. He would often break out in a cold sweat, as if feverish, staring at the ceiling, attempting to erase her from his mind. He tried to shred her image, rip it from his memories—that beloved face he would never see again, that warm body he would never touch—the warmth that had once scalded him as they sat a respectable distance apart on a shared bus seat.

Years later, he saw her name in a newspaper. The sharp stab of pain as he stared at her name was a sweet agony, cutting him deep. She had begun writing short stories, poems, and avant-garde literature. He was a literature student and accepted her as a practical science student. Why had it been so challenging to discover her likes and dislikes? Some people can't connect or click.

They were two strangers, failing miserably at the game of love. But wasn't it her fault, too? Her impatience and restlessness, her search for something impractical beyond the practical reality of his steadfast love for her? She hadn't given them the time to get to know each other better.

As more years passed, the pain receded like a tide. The memories dimmed to a hazy outline. He was moving on. It was amusing how long it took him to move on from a non-existent relationship that lasted six months.

One day, he saw her name in the paper again. Just after publishing her first and last novel in English, 'Mirage', she passed away from an illness. She had never married. The shock hit him like a wave welling up from long-lost depths, overwhelming his senses momentarily.

Had she ever found the love she sought? Or had she died still in search of it? He will never know. But one day, he will read her novel.

(i) There was a custom of forced elopement prevailing in Manipur in ancient times. A man could kidnap a woman that he wants and the tradition is that, the parents of the bride are informed the day after, and arrangements are undertaken for their marriage.

(ii) A humped bridge that spanned across the river Nambul.

Whispers in Isolation

It is sweet seeing the stars in her eyes
Someday, the bleak dawn might stare at her,
Mocking her for frayed dreams,
And pain might be her constant companion.

They met in December 2019 at the fitness club. She had joined for aerobics classes. He was tall and handsome, with broad shoulders that rippled with muscles. He wasn't into aerobics but came to work out at the gym, utilising equipment like the treadmill, stationary bike, dumbbells, foam rollers, stability balls, and plyometric boxes.

That day, she had hurried up the stairs, anxious about being late for her class. Meanwhile, he dashed down, having left his mobile phone in his car. They collided on the second-floor landing. She tumbled into a heap while he merely staggered. Regaining his composure, he offered, "I am so sorry; please let me help you up," extending his hand.

"It's okay, thanks," she declined, pushing herself up.

Their eyes met—hers black, his brown. Sparks flew, and both felt winded again.

"I had left my phone in the car, I think, so I was rushing to retrieve it," he explained. "I'm working out at the gym on the fourth floor. Can I walk you to your class?"

"It's okay. Thanks. I'm headed to the aerobics class on the third floor."

He felt reluctant to let her leave his life just like that. Not someone as beautiful and elegant as she was; he had never gazed into eyes as lovely as hers. "Please, allow me to accompany you. That fall might have hurt you," he implored, his brown eyes pleading as they gazed deeply into her dark ones.

Suddenly, she found herself wanting his company. "Okay," she agreed, and they ascended the staircase together.

"My name is Deepak. May I know yours?" he inquired.

"Pushpa," she replied softly.

"Wow, what a beautiful name," he commented.

"Thank you," she responded, a blush colouring her cheeks.

All too soon, they reached the landing of the third floor. She indicated the door to the Aerobics classroom. With reluctance, he escorted her to the door.

"Take care, Pushpa," he said as she looked back at him with beautiful dark eyes.

From that day forward, he seized every chance to be present on the stairs when she arrived for her class. She was punctual, always coming at exactly 4:20 PM for her classes that began at 4:30 PM. Initially, their exchanges were brief, limited to a cordial "Hi, it's nice to meet you again." It took some time for him to muster up the courage to ask for her phone number. One day, he did it. Her cheeks flamed at that simple exchange of phone numbers. From that day onwards, they frequently conversed over the phone and continued to meet daily on the stairs.

Neither could pinpoint the exact moment, but it was clear to both that they had fallen deeply in love.

"Pushpa, there hasn't been a single moment when I haven't thought of you. When will you come to my home to stay with me forever?" he inquired during one of their phone conversations.

"Deepak, we are still young; we must finish our studies and look for jobs. Once we have jobs, we are free to be together forever," she responded with a blend of pragmatism and affection.

"But that will take forever to be together forever. I can't wait that long," Deepak gushed.

"So if you can't wait, go find someone that can be with you now," Pushpa huffed.

"No, Pushpa, it's you or none," Deepak tried to soothe her.

Pushpa signed, "Then please be patient; we can't impose ourselves on our parents, though I know they can afford it, your parents; mine would blow their fuses if I eloped now."

His parents were doctors, her father was a teacher, and her mother was an ambitious housewife. They harboured grand ambitions for her, allowing her to choose her career path. She was pursuing her Bachelor of Science, with plans to continue on to a Master's degree and then a PhD, aspiring to become a college teacher in Imphal. Meanwhile, he was studying engineering in Bhopal and had returned home for the winter vacation. His parents had hoped he would follow in their footsteps, but he chose engineering.

Deepak's holiday was approaching, signalling it was time for him to return to his engineering college. However, the unexpected occurred: the Corona pandemic struck. India, along with all its states, was placed under lockdown. His institute transitioned to online classes. While he managed the theoretical components well, the practical sessions presented a challenge. These classes were designed for students to apply the theories learned in their courses to real-world scenarios, a task not easily replicated virtually.

Manipur, too, faced several phases of lockdown. Their fitness club had shut down, making it impossible for them to meet. Consequently, they began to communicate more frequently over the phone.

Deepak made a video call to her. As always, her eyes ignited a deep fire within him, and he yearned to be near her. "I long to meet you; please, just once, come outside."

Clutching her phone close, Pushpa responded, "Our home is quarantined; someone nearby succumbed to the coronavirus. As much as I want to, I'm sorry, but it's impossible."

Deepak sighed, "It's been so long since we've seen each other..."

An expression of intense sadness flitted across her face. "Yes, it's been two months since the lockdown started, but we meet daily, like now..."

"You know that's not enough... I need to feel you near me," he whispered huskily.

She felt the hot flame rising on her cheeks as she whispered, "One day soon... Oh, how I wish this pandemic would end."

From the background, her mother's piercing voice called, "Pushpa, why are you still on the phone? Enough is enough; hang up now."

She hugged the phone tightly and whispered as mists welled in her eyes,

"I love you, baby, see you, bye," Deepak mouthed.

The eyes staring at her from the screen seemed to burn into her soul as she hung up the phone.

♥

The call of love for young hearts can be hard to bear. She came out of her house one day at his request. All the restaurants were closed, so he took her on his bike to the countryside. His friend Gopal lived on the outskirts of Imphal in a place called Phubala. He lived with his old parents; no other person was in their household, as his parents had gone out to work in their field despite the lockdown restrictions, so he took the pair to his room in his house and discreetly left them alone.

They tried to chat to make up for the long separation. But, like the parched earth eagerly absorbing the first drops of rain, they gazed at each other with eyes that had been starved for each other's sight for too long. They were lost. Time ceased to exist; the earth seemed to pause, basking in the humid glow of the summer day.

When they regained their senses, they noticed the sun was setting; it was evening. It was too late to return home. Deepak's parents had come home after their day of work in the field, and there was no way Deepak could hide them. So, he had to tell his parents that his friends had eloped[i] .

Gopal's family informed Deepak's family, who then went to Pushpa's home for the formal ceremony called pao haidokpa, a custom in Manipur where after young people elope, the groom's parents call on the bride's parents and inform them about the eloping. They come together to discuss making preparations for the wedding.

When Deepak's family came to talk with Pushpa's parents, the latter were furious.

"Our daughter is still young; she has yet to complete her graduation; she can't be a simple housewife; she has a bright future ahead of her."

"Ibemma[ii] , we know that she can study after marriage." Her father, Doctor Suresh, tried to console Pushpa's mother.

"Taibungo[iii], please give us some time; please bring our daughter back home."

"As you wish, Ibemma, but young people should not stay long at home after eloping; it is best to arrange their marriage soon."

"Taibungo, we will talk to our daughter first."

So, Pushpa was brought home. Her mother looked piercingly at her daughter as she said, "You are so young, Pushpa; why didn't you use your logic? He is also still studying; you will depend on his parents and be at their mercy; why couldn't you have waited a few more years?"

Pushpa bowed low as she murmured, "I am so sorry, Mother."

Whatever Pushpa's parents' reservations were, keeping their daughter at home long after an elopement was not good, so arrangements were made to meet Deepak's parents again to plan their wedding.

♥

It was the third day after the elopement when Pushpa received the news from Deepak. His friend Arun, along with his parents, tested positive for COVID. Therefore, he had also gotten himself tested. Results were due that day. He insisted that she should also get tested. Pushpa went alone to Babina Diagnostics and got her tests done. Later that evening, she heard from Deepak that he had tested positive; the dinner they had shared at Arun's home that evening had proven to be their undoing. Pushpa also tested positive the next day. Luckily, she didn't develop a fever, as she was one of the asymptomatic ones. However, Deepak developed a high fever and was hospitalised. Despite her agony and desperation, Pushpa couldn't meet or comfort him in his illness due to the prevailing restrictions regarding COVID-19. His mother stayed at his bedside as his condition deteriorated. He died ten days after their elopement.

Pushpa collapsed upon hearing the news.

"No, Deepak, no.........please", were her last words as she swooned.

No family members attended Deepak's funeral. Hired people wrapped his body in plastic and burnt him at a makeshift pyre, as was the norm then. Family members were not allowed to perform the funeral of a person who had passed away due to COVID-19. Pushpa tried her best to find out where his body was cremated, but she was not successful.

Deepak's mother remained in quarantine for about 15 more days, but luckily, she never developed the virus. However, she would gladly have died in her son's stead, for no woman ought ever to grieve for the death of their offspring. The two women grieved for the same person: one with a mother's poignant love for her son, the other with an agonised yearning for her lost love.

Pushpa's heart remained a vast ocean of emptiness, a poignant reminder of the love she had known and the future that will never be. Deepak's mother will always feel an empty ache in heart that will forever mourn the loss of her son,

== Endnotes ==

(i) In Manipur, eloping (chenba) is a tradition where the boy and the girl (who have been in love for some time) stay together away from their families for a night at another place, such as a friend's place, relatives' place, or even a hotel in modern times. This is known as "NUPI CHENBA" (meaning eloping with the girl with the intention of getting married). Such a tradition is accepted in Manipur. The following day, the boy's parents will come to the girl's family with relatives and close friends to discuss the wedding arrangement.
(ii) Formal address to a younger woman.
(iii) Respectful address to an older man.

4

A Second Chance at love

Her heart was a desert, her eyes empty,
Into her heart, he slowly enters,
Past sorrows fade, hope shines brightly,
'Take a chance again', a voice whispers.

Her hand was busy peeling the potatoes and cutting them into tiny oblong pieces, intricately involved in its task with unconscious volition. However, her mind drifted in search of lost horizons, the long-lost dreams that had once infused her with life in her youth. Déjà vu assailed her senses; she saw again, as if, in real, the beauty of the rainbow of colours painting her heart while her mind climbed the highest heights and plumbed the deepest depths on the wings of love.

She had tasted all nuances of love when she was with him- the only man- who could touch the innermost core of her being, the man who could read her mind like a book and decipher the meaning of the butterfly expressions flitting across her face.

Her dreams died with him.

"I will always be there for you," he had whispered in her ear when they sat together, engrossed in each other, oblivious to the world around them, on the spacious lawn of the war cemetery in the heartland of Imphal. The flowers blooming in profusion nodded in agreement.

They had met as if by magic, as they moved along pre-ordained paths, as if aware of each other's existence, even before they knew each other in this lifetime. They were destined to meet and to love. They were meant to be together, filling each other with peace and well-being. This is love, she had thought giddily the first time their eyes met—love as she had always dreamed of.

They were young and deeply in love. The fires of passion never burned as bright in any heart other than theirs. They were inseparable. One soul, two bodies: linked by an invisible cord, enhancing their extraordinary mental communion. He would suddenly call just as she was thinking about calling him. They could read each other's thoughts and complete each other's sentences. They were two very familiar persons from previous lives meeting again in this life in unfamiliar garb. They were twin souls, destined for each other across space and time, waiting for reunion through centuries of lifetimes for karmic soul testing separates them in many lifetimes.

Even God must have envied them and their unique bond. Or was it the Evil Eye? It must be their karmic soul testing. Her dreams vaporised into pungent nightmares. Crossfire between C.R.P.F personnel and insurgents took him away from her. Forever.

The years accumulated in layers, folding her skin into tiny little crevices that taunted her whenever she managed to muster up the courage to look seriously at her soulless reflection. Always...empty eyes had stared back at an immovably stone-cold image.

She finished her engineering course...in limbo. She was a numb and frozen entity walking through the lanes and by-lanes of life without noticing its immense beauty. But once she got her job, a tiny spark was ignited. Her career became her life. She strove to be known for her 'brain' in a male-dominated profession.

One day, she got a marriage proposal from a family closely linked with her own; their parents were friends, and he was a college lecturer at a reputable college in Imphal. Lata had known him for a long time but just as a family friend.

Their parents arranged for them to meet and share their thoughts. They sat in her beautiful garden, surrounded by blooming flowers. Sitting beside him, she said, "Our marriage is arranged for practical reasons; I have always thought of you more like a brother. Love was never a part of the equation; would that be enough for you?"

Kanta, who had loved her for ages, replied, "True, but perhaps love for me can grow in your heart.... like these flowers..."

Lata smiled quizzically, but she knew she could never love again...

She accepted the proposal, for she knew he would treat her well. She respected his calm manner and gentleness. He had one quality that she noticed: self-confidence. He was not envious of her career and its success. He was such a far cry from the insecure, chauvinistic males she usually sees in their small, conservative society, so she accepted the proposal. They were married with much pomp and ceremony.

She was here now as his bride, performing the expected feminine chores as an obedient and dutiful wife.

"Lata, now what are you dreaming of? Alice in wonderland, is it?' her husband's teasing voice cut into her reverie.

"Oh...!" startled, she picked up the knife which had slipped from her frozen fingers. She willed her mind to concentrate on preparing the vegetables for cooking.

Why did only women have to deal with the demands of both career and household? She really must get Kanta to find help. She mused while her husband watched her gently, embarrassing her as always with his attention.

"Lata, you have to go to your office. Won't you be late?" her husband asked worriedly.

"No- it will be okay. I can finish everything within one hour."

"Oh...you can cook that fast; let me help you", he said, with a smile lighting up the craggy features of his generous face. He picked up the knife and started peeling the potatoes.

"No, no, what will people say?" Lata tried to take away the knife from his hand, but he didn't budge.

Then, her mother-in-law Maipakpi, who had just entered the room, said, "Kanta, what are you doing here? Go to your room. I will help Lata".

Lata blushed at her mother-in-law's words, but Kanta was unfazed, "It's an old-fashioned notion, Ima, that you think a man shouldn't help their wives; we are all human beings; we are the same; she also needs help".

"You can help her when I am not around or sick in bed, but not while I am alive and well", Maipakpi insisted.

She shooed him away, and Kanta made a face at his mother as he left the kitchen.

She had to smile at such childlike innocence in a grown man but worried about what people might say about him. Meitei society is quite conservative, and men who helped their wives with feminine chores were dubbed hen-pecked.

She found her husband to be unlike any man she had encountered before. He was not ashamed of being seen doing 'womanly' tasks. Helping people was an inborn need in him. So, helping his wife with household chores in small ways came naturally to him. He was secure enough, confident enough to be uncaring of being dubbed 'henpecked.'

The months passed slowly. It was a gentle voyage of discovery for her. Over the few months she had known him, she discovered that her husband was kind, considerate, helpful, and gentle with everyone.

He wasn't very romantic or as acutely aware of her emotions as her lost love had been. But he is such a good man: kind and considerate; what more could a woman ask for? Passion? But passion dims with the lengthening shadows of time. Romance? Romance dies with the over-familiarity of living together.

One day, he came home from college a bit disturbed. "Lata, I have been asked to take the students of my class for an external excursion to Darjeeling. They fixed it so suddenly. We will leave the day after tomorrow. It is a journey of 10 days".

Lata felt a queer feeling grow in her chest, a tightness. She was now in the 7th month of pregnancy and needed him with her; they had not been apart for even one day, for almost eight months now.

"Oh, okay, let me see what clothes you will take; I will wash them for you".

"I won't carry much; don't tire yourself out", he quipped as he helped her choose the clothes.

After he was gone, Lata felt the emptiness strike her with full force. She waited for him to call. And he did once he reached Darjeeling, "Dear, I miss you; I hope my mother is helping you with the tasks? You must not work too much".

Radha felt tears sting her eyes, "I am fine; you must be exhausted with the journey too. Rest well!".

He rang every night for the next ten days. They talked about everything under the Sun. She missed him so much. Her heart leapt with pleasure when the tour bus dropped him home on the 11th day.

That night, it was stormy; the two sat side by side on their small double bed and talked while the torrential rain lashed at their window as if trying to get in. The feeble glow of the lantern cast a shimmering, ethereal glow over their room.

He sat absorbing the beauty of her soft, fragile features, the large, questioning eyes, the small pert nose and the soft, kissable mouth that had never once responded to his caresses or entreaties.

She stared wonderingly at her husband, meeting his gaze and feeling a butterfly flapping its wings in the corner of her heart for the first time in years since....

"Oh, it's scary the way it suddenly started raining today, though it is not the rainy season yet; I am so scared of what might have been if the rain had come before your bus reached Imphal."

"Are you worried for me?" Kanta looked enquiringly into her eyes.

She blushed red and looked down.

"Never worry, I will always come home to you.", he spoke as he gently touched the soft swell of the new life and looked enquiringly into her eyes.

"If it is a girl, I will call her Shakhenbi. That's a nice name, isn't it?"

"Um! What if it is a boy?" She gazed adoringly into his ardent eyes as she lightly placed her hand over his.

"Then you choose."

"Shakhenba", she volunteered.

"That is very good". A simple, uncomplicated joy lit up his eyes.

"We have to start saving right away for her. I shall ask ..."

"Him!" She interrupted teasingly.

"Her! For you! And I hope she looks like you. I will ask my L.I.C. and post office savings agents about any schemes for young children".

Her husband was already planning for their as-yet-unborn child. She beamed with pleasure, newly discovered. A soft, secure feeling suffused her heart.

"Lata, I have loved you from the first time that I set eyes on you. But all the time we have been together, you have never admitted to any feelings for me. Don't you care at all?"

He looked at her with a tender light in his eyes. Though there was no grudge against her in those eyes, she saw a hint of hurt in them for the first time since they had been together. She felt the mist welling up in hers. She reached out blindly and found his rough, unshaven cheeks with her trembling hands.

"You are the best husband a woman could ever have. Why shouldn't I care? I do care".

Yes. She cared, for she loved him. She would always love him. Deeply, achingly. Not the romantic, wild, passionate love of her past, but with gentle care and concern. This was a gentle fire that would burn softly through the years and warm her winter years. Not a raging flame that would burn itself out after a short fiery burst. Nor a fiery storm that would uproot her existence.

But this is also love. Sure, steady love. Outside, the storm hissed and spat. When the lantern was extinguished, it became pitch dark. But she slept securely beside him. The storm would spend itself. She was safe.

5

The Unplanned Bond

Her mind calls him 'enemy',
Her heart calls him 'love',
From passion to animosity
From animosity to passion.
A story of contradictions.

Ningthibi had been living in limbo since a reckless driver tragically ended her fiancé's life. As an electrical engineer, she had ascended to the role of Executive Engineer of the electricity department in her small town. Her position commanded overwhelming respect from men, who maintained a respectful distance.

Now, she was 35 years old, nine years since the accident. A mere mention of the incident was enough to shatter her. Her grief persisted like a raw, throbbing wound, casting a dull, grey pall over her world, enveloping her life in darkness. Then, Korou entered her life, a bright ray of sunshine illuminating the dark corners of her existence.

He introduced slivers of light into her shadowed world. He was all noise and brightness; in contrast, she was silence and shadow. A self-taught electrician, he had been released from prison for a crime he inadvertently committed, serving six years. She was curious but shrugged off her curiosity, thinking it is best if the past is laid to rest.

"Madam, thank you for putting in a good word for me in my selection." he smiled, his eyes crinkling at the corners.

"You're welcome. I can sense that you are an honest man; you also performed well in the interview," she replied. She instantly liked him, sensing an aura of innocence surrounding him, as if he had never done anything wrong. She found it hard to believe he had ever been jailed, and although he attempted to explain, she never desired to learn the nature of his crime.

Ningthibi observed Korou's diligent work ethic and transformation into a reliable, dependable, honest, and sincere employee. Instinctively, she placed her trust in him. An unlikely friendship blossomed between the Executive Engineer and the Electrician. She refrained from inquiring about his past, although he revealed that he had committed a serious crime, possibly murder.

Ningthibi interrupted him, insisting, "Please, don't disclose your mistakes in the past; leave them behind.... I'm convinced it must be some mistake; I can't imagine you intentionally harming anyone." Her trusting words revived his faith, fostering his healing. She helped him lay the past to rest, and in turn, he helped her in getting over her grief for her lost love.

♥

Over time, Korou became an integral part of her life. Ningthibi adored his smile; when he grinned, the corners of his eyes crinkled, and his eyes seemed to vanish. She grew fond of his eyes, which were lovely, warm, and vibrant, enhancing his features. His smile was captivating; his lips would stretch, revealing a set of sparkling white, even, and clean teeth. She couldn't get enough of seeing his smile; somehow, she felt complete when he did. He playfully teased her, gesturing with his hands to draw her laughter. Life had suddenly changed — from the dull, dreary agony of going through the motions— to the joy of looking forward each day to see a young man's smile. Why did his smile move her so? She wished that he would smile always, that nothing, no one, should ever hurt him or wipe that smile away from his face.

Was she falling in love with her junior in the department? How could she? She was his superior. And more importantly— she would love her fiancé forever. She tried hard to deny the giddy feeling that rose within her whenever Korou smiled, the butterflies that fluttered in her heart, for she still clung to memories of her deceased lover. How could she ever betray him? It was turmoil anew as she believed she would love him eternally. But she couldn't help enjoying her moments with Korou, who brought laughter and fun into her life.

Happiness could never last for Ningthibi. One day, it left her after turning her world upside down. She was scouring through some old newspapers filed by her assistant for some news about her department when she saw a newspaper she had never tried to read before, a news report that revealed the name of the man who went to trial for hitting and killing the love of her life. The shock hit her like a lightning bolt; she called Korou over and asked if the man in the newspaper was him. Korou said yes. He recounted what had happened that day.

♥

He was driving home from a school reunion. He was a teetotaller, but his friends had made him drink a glass of whisky. The unfamiliar liquid coursed through his veins, making him feel dizzy, warm, and sleepy. All he wanted to do was lie down and sleep, but his sick mother waited for him at home, and he had to go to her. Once or twice, the car dangerously swerved and almost crashed against the cemented embankments on the side of the road. With tired eyes struggling against sleep, his vehicle came careening along the road; the light had changed to red, but he didn't notice and didn't stop. There was a sickening thud as the car crashed into someone who had crossed the pedestrian walkway. The person was thrown some five feet ahead and lay in a crumpled heap. Horrified, Korou stopped the car, and with numb legs that refused to obey his commands, he walked over to the figure lying in a pool of his own blood.

The man was already dead. Korou had been jailed and served six years; his dream of becoming an electrical engineer faded into the mist. His mother also passed away during his imprisonment, leaving him without family upon release. He had only completed his secondary education—he struggled to find employment. After selling his parents' fields and retaining just a tiny plot for his homestead, he pursued a diploma course as an electrician, juggling part-time jobs to support his studies. He has now secured his diploma, but his prison record impeded his search for a job.

When a job listing in the electricity department appeared in the gazette, he applied, albeit with little expectation of success. He effortlessly passed the written examination, but there were rumours in these times that one has to grease the hands of the powers that be to secure your post in an interview; he couldn't do that. However, during the interview, the department head—a beautiful woman with soulful sad eyes—gazed intently at him, saw into his soul and said one good word for him; that was how he got selected.

Upon realising that Korou was the one responsible for taking away the love of her life, Ningthibi's long-suppressed emotions shimmered to the surface and burst forth. Her heart throbbed with pain as rage assailed every fibre of her being. "Did you ever stop to think about the people from whom you took him?" she demanded.

Shocked eyes stared back at her in wonder. "Madam, are you related to him?"

"Silence! He was my fiancé; we were to be married in two months," she retorted.

Tears glistened in his eyes and streamed unchecked down his face as he gazed upon the delicate features of the person he had learned to love, now transfigured by mad hate, who screamed at him, "Leave! Get out of here and never come near me again!"

Ningthibi now felt an emotion in her heart, which she could only construe as hate for Korou. He had killed her fiancé twice. The first time by taking his life and the second time by erasing his memory from her mind. His loved face was fading from her recollection. She did everything she could to avoid Korou, even ensuring his transfer to another department so that she may see less of him.

Despite her resolve to put as much space between Kourou and herself, Ningthibi's deceitful heart refused to give up the imprint of memories—shared laughter, stolen glances, and beautiful moments together. His smile had warmed her soul like a sunbeam breaking through storm clouds.

Memories of a fateful day flooded her mind— a day filled with happiness, as she didn't know the truth of his past then. They had shared tea and snacks at a small hotel far away from the prying eyes of their colleagues, and he had dared to tell her amidst the smiles and laughter of their happiness in just being together:

"I like you, Madam", he had said, his voice trembling with vulnerability. She had been taken aback, her heart racing. But before she could respond, he apologised, regret sketching lines on his face. "I am sorry, Madam, I shouldn't have dared to voice my feelings to you," he murmured.

His confession of his feelings had disturbed the equilibrium of their relationship for a few days, but Ningthibi felt herself responding to it like a sunflower opening out to the sun's warm rays. Her once-frozen heart was beginning to thaw out.

And then, like a cruel twist of fate, the truth emerged. The man she had loved—the one who had filled her days with joy— was snatched from her by the man who now stood before her. His memory, too, had been stolen, erased by him.

Ningthibi's anger simmered, a tempest brewing within her. "I hate you!" she wanted to scream. "You killed him twice— once in body and now in memory. May you rot in hell!"

Her desire for vengeance consumed her. She envisioned ways to make him suffer: terminate his job, throw him into a cold, unforgiving cell, or perhaps even run a car into him. Anything to mirror the pain she had endured.

Yet, it was as if fate conspired to make them cross paths again, like two planets bound by gravity.

On the narrow corridor between the two office sections — one where she worked and the other where she had posted him—they met again, and their eyes met. His gaze held remorse, and he stepped closer, his voice barely audible. "Madam," he began, "I am sorry for the pain I have caused you. Please forgive me. I miss you."

Ningthibi's fury surged. She raised her hand, the slap echoing through the corridor. "Stay away from me," she spat.

"I hate you." And as he winced, she revelled in the pain mirrored in his eyes.

♥

It was 25th January, and preparations were on for the Republic Day parade the next day. Each government department erected pandals on the roads. A particular underground group had called a bandh, but the departments had to participate. Ningthibi was busy in her office, engaged in paperwork for the upcoming preparations, when she saw Korou chatting happily with the new clerk in her office. He was speaking, and she was laughing merrily. Some fierce emotion rose in her heart as she saw them. She rang a bell, and Priya came running in.

"Priya, have you finished typing what I gave you earlier?"

Nervously, Priya replied, "Yes, Madam. It's almost done".

Ningthibi spoke sternly. "Priya, there is so much work to be done; you must not waste time in this office chatting with people. Go and do your job".

Priya was stunned; she had not wasted any time or done anything wrong but replied obediently, "Yes, Madam, I will return to my task!".

After Priya left the office room, Ningthibi tried to calm down. What was that for? What is wrong with her? She felt terribly ashamed of her behaviour. When she went out, Priya was busy at her desk, and Korou had gone away, perhaps to his section of the office.

Days later, she saw him relaxing with his friends after work at the office. He laughed and smiled as if he had no care in the world. Transfixed, she stared at the smile on the face that she hated—the smile she could never forget. An expression of happiness interspersed with sadness flitted across her face. She realised the hate in her heart had gone; she no longer hated seeing him happy. Instead, she felt a tinge of happiness in her heart, seeing how happy he looked. At the same time, she also felt sad that she could never share in that happiness. The hate was gone; she had forgiven him. He caught her gaze, came over, and tried to say something, but she turned abruptly and walked briskly away. Pain contorted his face. He hurried after her, "Madam, Priya is my cousin. My aunt's daughter". Ningthibi felt her cheeks burn, but she stopped, whirled around, faced him and said, "I am not interested!". Then she turned and hurried away, her heart thudding painfully in her chest.

Months passed: months when life became dull and dreary again for Ningthibi. The hate that she tried to dredge up in her heart for Korou was gone. Instead, there was an ache, a need to see his smile again. One day, she was driving to the office in her car, preoccupied with her thoughts. She remembered his words, "I like you, Madam". She didn't realise that the light had turned red and was still speeding when she saw someone stepping on the road a few meters ahead. She stepped on her brakes and turned the wheel away from the person ahead, missing him by a few inches. At the last moment, she knew it was him: her enemy, her love.

She stopped the car and walked back to where he stood shaken. Uncaring of the vehicles that honked on the road shouting at her to park her car in a proper place, she walked up to him. He stood before her, safe and smiling. Relief flooded her heart...so much relief and happiness she couldn't breathe.

He smiled at her, his eyes disappearing from his face again, "Madam, why did you swerve? You should just have run me over; that way, I would be punished eternally for the pain I have caused you".

Reaction set in. Ningthibi reached out, grabbed Korou's arm and shouted at him, her voice rising to a crescendo as she spoke... "No, don't ever say that! You must never die! Do you understand? You cannot die. You must live on beside me! Say that you will never die.! Say that you will live on beside me". Tears were streaming unchecked down her cheeks...

"Yes, I will live on beside you".... Korou mouthed... amazement suffused with joy lighting up his craggy features.

An infinitely tender expression came over her face as she looked into his eyes... "Korou...today... I know now what I feel for you.... I love you...."

With his face depicting an almost painful joy and his heart in his eyes, Korou stepped forward...The sun was behind them as their silhouettes intertwined.

6

The Gift of Love

The greatest gift of all:

The gift of love,

It asks not for possession,

No gilded cage or key binds it,

Friends, parents or lovers,

It is the giver's purest joy.

The hospital room was dreary and dim. Moisture clung to the walls from water seeping from the bathrooms above. The air was heavy with the musty scent of disinfectant, which spoke of medicine, decay, and illness. In the corner lay a bed that seemed too large for the room, its presence almost oppressive. Upon it rested a figure so slight she appeared practically ethereal. A slender girl slept soundly on the bed, adorned with luxuriant long eyelashes, a small pert nose, and full warm lips. She lay there, an embodiment of vulnerability, connected to the world of the living by the slender lifeline of an intravenous drip.

Beside the bed, on the stool, sat a dignified middle-aged woman. Worry lines were etched on her once flawless features,

75

and her eyes were moist, as if she were fighting back tears. Hers was a face marked by unexpressed pain and sadness. She watched over the girl with an intensity that conveyed deep care and concern.

Tampha, the staff nurse assigned to the special ward of RIMS (Regional Institute of Medical Sciences), came quietly into the room and had a whispered consultation with the woman, who got up and left the room slowly. Tenderly tucking away the stray wisps of hair falling across the girl's forehead, Tampha nudged her, "Wake up, Dina....!"

The sleeping girl opened her huge, haunted eyes to stare at the sweet-looking nurse. "Um... What is it? Where is Ima[i] and Tamo[ii] Sushil?"

"Ima has just stepped out to speak with another patient, her friend, in the next room. And your brother Sushil has gone to his office. Now, relax. Guess who is waiting outside, eager to see you?"

"Who? Tell me!" The sick girl asked in an anxious whisper, seeming to perk up with life.

"Pradip..." At the mention of that name, the sick girl stiffened. The name seemed to strike her almost physically, robbing her of breath, yet she remained silent, expectant.

Tampha continued, "Pradip...your Pradip! He is a doctor in the surgery department of this hospital. I didn't want to tell you earlier. I wanted to surprise you".

Too stunned and very profoundly moved, the sick girl made a visible effort to pull herself together and managed to murmur, "I am frightened; what did you tell him about me...?"

"I mentioned your name to him, and he told me how much he loved you; he loves you still". If Dina had looked closely at her friend Tampha's face, she would have wondered at the sad expression on the usually cheerful face, the struggle to smile. She was wrapped up in her unexpected happiness and didn't notice the expressions flitting across her friend's face.

"It can't be. Is that possible after all these years..."? Dina whispered.

"Yes..." Tampha seemed to choke and turned away from Dina suddenly, but she shook her head slightly and said with effort. "Come, let's spruce you up. Let me comb your hair. She tidied up the young woman's unruly hair. Then she said, with a nervous, anxious expression, "Doctor, please come in."

Adorned in a doctor's gown, a tall, thin young man entered the room quietly. His features were impeccable- a face like a Greek deity, complemented by his jet-black, curly hair. Upon his arrival, Tampha rose and silently retreated to a corner. The girl on the bed forced herself up and sat on her bed, fixing her intense gaze upon the figure now standing beside her. Her frank, open stare unsettled the young man, causing him to shift nervously, at a loss for words. Then, breaking the silence, the girl whispered, "You have come. I knew you would..."

The words seemed to melt the frost encasing the young man's heart, prompting him, in a voice laden with emotion, to respond, "Dina... I am so sorry...!"

"Hush! Please don't say anything more," whispered the sick girl, signalling for silence and beckoning him to sit on the stool; he complied willingly. Time seemed to stand still. The sick girl's eyes, wide open, lingered on the young man's face with an intensity that might have been deemed 'forward' in a healthy woman. It was as though she was attempting to memorise every feature until, finally, with a visible effort, she composed herself and spoke. "I wanted so much to meet you again... Oh, how I prayed... I wanted to tell you so much...!" She paused, a blush colouring her pale cheeks. He waited patiently; gathering her strength, she confessed, "I have always loved you." Tears followed her admission. Her candid, pitiful confession and the tears that flowed freely resonated with a deeply buried chord in the young man's heart. He rose from his stool and sat on her bed, and genuine words spilt from his lips: "I loved you too!" He reached out, gently touching her hair. She stiffened initially, but then, suddenly, she leaned into his embrace; he held her close as she wept. What else could he do when someone so vulnerable was surrendering herself to him so completely, without any barriers? Someone who had once erected so many barriers he couldn't cross was now open, vulnerable, and exposed. Night had turned to day. It was like the sun revolved around the earth, not vice versa. Tampha, standing silently in the corner, quickly left the room, wiping the tears streaming down her cheeks.

♥

He came every day with a bouquet of freshly picked flowers. Dina seemed to come to life with each of his visits. She chatted animatedly, sharing stories about herself and eagerly inquiring about his life during their time apart. She embraced with fervour the unexpected joy that had entered her life. Her mother, brother, Tampha, and the other nurses tactfully gave them privacy, immersing them in their little world. Ten days after his first visit, Dina passed away. At just 28 years old, a serene smile graced her lifeless features; in death, she had found peace. She left behind a heartbroken mother and elder brother. On the day of her passing, Tampha was beyond consolation. The young doctor seemed to diminish, becoming a shadow of himself as if withdrawing into his depths.

Much later, Tampha allowed herself to reminisce. The new patient had just been admitted, and it was a complete shock to discover that it was Dina—her childhood best friend and confidant during their school years. They were inseparable back then, sharing stories and secrets. The other girls envied them, even nicknaming them Laurel and Hardy. Tampha was plump, boisterous, and outgoing—an effervescent extrovert— while Dina was thin, lean, and introverted, a painfully shy mouse.

Dina possessed a hauntingly exotic face that promised future beauty, whereas Tampha might be considered plain. However, any allure Dina had paled compared to the sheer joy emanating from Tampha's sunny smile, which was a constant presence, casting a glow on her features and causing dimples to dance across her cheeks.

They were like light and shadow, stark contrasts in character, yet they created a complete entity in unison. For Dina, other friends were nonexistent. She was a timid mouse, unconsciously and involuntarily recoiling from social interaction. Everyone wondered what Tampha saw in Dina; Dina was virtually invisible to them. She lacked a voice and a discernible personality, existing only as a silent shadow next to the radiant Tampha. Only Tampha could coax Dina to speak; only Tampha had access to the secrets hidden in Dina's silent depths and witnessed her quiet, gentle sense of humour.

After completing their 12th standard together, Tampha ventured to Coimbatore to pursue her BSc in Nursing, while Dina went for a Bachelor of Honors Degree course in English at Chandigarh University. Time and distance had slowly eroded the bond between the once inseparable pair. Their relationship had dwindled to a mere exchange of cards on Birthdays. Today, they were meeting again in a hospital room. And gentle Dina was dying. No medicine could cure her. No power on earth could save her. A sad pitiful life that was ending before it could be lived.

Tampha felt the strange need to stay near them even when her hospital shift ended. She remained steadfast in her care, managing Dina's medications, overseeing her IV infusions, and maintaining a tireless vigil near her friend's bedside. It seemed a compulsion to offer all she could, pouring her heart into the care of her gravely ill friend.

♥

Memories of her conversations with Dina haunted Tampha...

"I am dying, Tampha; it's only a matter of weeks... maybe days," Dina had said with a resignation that chilled the air. Tampha couldn't bear to hear any more, "Shh, Dina, you'll be fine. Never lose hope... We're here for you."

"But it's the truth; what's there to hope for? I'm not naive, Tampha. The day I was diagnosed, I knew..."

"Please, Dina, people have overcome fatal diseases before. Medical literature is filled with real-life stories of miraculous recoveries... keep faith." Tampha attempted to offer comfort, but Dina persisted, "It's too late for me, Tampha. Acceptance brings me peace; don't give me false hope... My only wish is for Ima not to suffer too much... I pray Tamo Sushil takes good care of her..." Tears streamed down her cheeks. Tampha reached out with her handkerchief, murmuring consolations, barely aware of her words, "It's okay... it's okay... if only you had told me about your illness sooner..."

Dina brushed Tampha's hand aside, irritation lacing her voice, "What should I have written? That I'm sick, dying? I don't want pity, not even from you, Tampha. I'm tired of it; no one needs pity."

Those words wounded Tampha deeply. She also felt a pang of guilt... How had they grown so distant? One must cling to the irreplaceable—true friendship, love. Had Dina confided in her sooner, while the disease was still nascent, perhaps Tampha could have found a way to help her... It was wishful thinking, but she still wished she had known earlier...

Over the following days, Tampha noticed a transformation in Dina. She became more animated and alive as if shedding the years of silence, timidity and withdrawal. Her illness sapped her vitality, but she exhibited newfound vivacity that was almost alarming to Tampha.

Dina was grasping at life with desperation, compensating for the lost years. It seemed she was truly beginning to live at the very moment life was slipping away.

Yet, despite her liveliness, Tampha felt Dina was concealing something deep within. Something significant and intense. Dina seldom spoke of her life in Chandigarh; she would begin to share, then abruptly retreat into silence, piquing Tampha's curiosity. She yearned to learn more.

On that unforgettable day, Tampha entered the hospital, carrying a bouquet freshly picked from her garden and gently roused Dina from her afternoon slumber. "Sleepyhead, look what I've brought for you today..." Dina, a lover of flowers, squealed with delight. "They're beautiful, thank you, Tampha. How can I ever thank you enough to show my gratitude?"

"Tell me about Chandigarh. You're concealing something; share it with me... friends shouldn't keep secrets."

Dina blushed. "You're astute, Tampha... but you're right, no more secrets... though, truthfully, there's nothing much to tell!"

"I sense there's more... please, tell me," Tampha implored.

"All my life, I've felt an emptiness, Tampha, constantly searching for something to fill the void... and for a brief period, something did... until..."

"You must tell me," Tampha urged, insistent.

"It is the story of my life, Tampha—a tale of unrequited longings. I was a drifter without ambition, yearning for only one thing: love—a passionate, all-consuming love. I desired it so intensely... but..."

"But? What?" Tampha's curiosity intensified.

"It's a fundamental truth: never crave something too fervently. If you do, it will elude you. Even when it seems within reach, the fear of losing it will drive it away... That's what happened to me, Tampha. I longed for love so desperately that when it finally approached, I recoiled... I cast it aside, Tampha."

Dina had lapsed into silence after that speech. Later, after much persuasion, she confided in Tampha, "Tampha, I have never truly lived; I've only existed. I've always refrained from indulging myself due to my fear of consequences. If I desperately wanted to purchase something, I wouldn't if it was costly. If I yearned to go out and enjoy with my friends, like when they would call out to me, beckoning from the lawns of my hostel to join them for antakshari[iii] because I sang well—in the bathroom, that is—I would hide in my room and pretend not to hear. I was too shy and scared of embarrassing myself. I longed to join the girls from my hostel when they attended hostel nights at the boys' hostels, supervised by the hostel staff... but I held back. I wanted to accompany them to parties and other social events... but I never did. I was a social misfit, a tongue-tied, pathetic fool. I ran away from life. Now, my life feels over before it has even begun." She sighed deeply with regret, and the weight of her unfulfilled life seemed to transfer to the cheerful Tampha, who sat beside Dina and sighed softly.

Dina continued, "I fled from love—the only love of my life. It happened during my final year of college. He was an intern at PGIMER Chandigarh. Our paths crossed on a journey," she recounted, inhaling deeply the memories that danced in the thick haze of her drug-clouded mind. This time, no urging from Tampha was needed for her to continue.

"I was heading home for the summer break with the other Manipuri girls from college. He was returning home with a group of Manipuri guys studying in Chandigarh, and the girls knew some of the boys, so they teamed up and travelled home together. Perhaps my shyness struck a chord with him. I always felt out of place among those lively, chirpy girls who often teased me, making me the target of their jokes—not that I held it against them. My shyness was almost pitiable. Initially, he might have felt sorry for me," she paused, then with a decisive shake of her head, "No, it wasn't pity... I first became aware of him—or rather his presence—when I struggled with my heavy suitcase on the railway platform, and he lingered nearby, seemingly eager to relieve me of my load, yet unable to do so as he juggled two hefty suitcases himself."

"Then...?" Tampha leaned in, her curiosity piqued, eager to hear more.

"On that journey, there were subtle moments... like when he defended me as the other girls teased me, his anger flaring on my behalf... or when he brought me food as I sat alone— minor events to some, but monumental to a solitary heart".

"His presence enveloped me, always there... protective... We shared a silent intimacy as if he could perceive every emotion, every mood of mine, as though we had been intimately acquainted in past lives... "

We had travelled to Guwahati by train, but we were to take the Air India flight home from Guwahati. At Guwahati airport, as I sat alone while my companions went to gaze at the airport stalls— he came and sat beside me, not saying a single word, but he placed a comic book on his lap, and I could see the words on the book: 'Love of my Life'....It touched me, but we never said a word to each other...These memories, I later realised vividly, and when I acknowledged my love for him, that realisation became my tragedy..."

"What happened?" Tampha pressed, but after those words, Dina clammed up, refusing to divulge more. Driven by curiosity, Tampha continued to prod her in the following days.

Ultimately, she made Dina open up again. But there was no story; there was only an ending.

"He used to come to our college, even to hang around at the gate of our hostel... He came to our hostel nights: get-togethers organised between boy's and girl's colleges. He came to every event of our college. When I realised that he was as much in love with me as I was in love with him, my first emotions were overwhelming happiness...he haunted my thoughts; he filled up my life completely. But...my fear of losing that love came in the way... I never got to tell him Tampha....'

Dina's voice had quivered. "Tampha, I had always been afraid of men and shied away from their presence; I yearned for love, but I was also scared of it... though I wanted it so desperately... and when I saw love in his eyes...I started avoiding him like the plague; I ran away from his presence even though I yearned to stay. I was so scared of my feelings and his rejection that I ran away. How I longed to stay, but I couldn't. My treacherous feet took me away from him..." The tears had come like a flood. "But I can never run away from those memories, from the love that was mine if it wasn't for my shyness...he still haunts my memories..."

Dina burst into deep, wrenching sobs as Tampha held her. Guilt consumed her, too; she had opened a Pandora's box of emotions. Tears filled her eyes as she listened to the sad voice crying out for a lost love—an ephemeral love, but more important than life to the lonely soul. It might be just her imagination intensifying her emotions in the loneliness of her timid life... but then perhaps, if she had not let it slip away, that love might have been hers—a love that was her only chance, a wasted chance, to find true happiness in her short life. Perhaps, fortified with 'his love,' she would have had the will to live, fight against her illness, and conquer it. Perhaps... 'Perhaps' is such a flimsy word. Why was Dina so insecure? She was not poor. Her father had left her landed properties and a steady source of income from well-made investments; she was also beautiful. Because of her fears and her nameless insecurities, she had created an impenetrable wall around herself, stunting her personality, stifling her life, and condemning her to a haunted, lonely existence. And now, this disease was consuming her body while shyness had sapped her spirit. It was the story of a sad, pathetic life; it was so very unfair that she had to die with so much unfulfilled longing — without having fully lived her life.

Another nostalgic memory unfolded in Tampha's mind. She implored the handsome young doctor, "Doctor, please go to her. She needs you!" His response was stern, "Don't play the martyr. She doesn't need your pity!" She countered passionately, "It's not pity. Every human being deserves a bit of happiness. She has never been happy. Please, make her happy!"

He looked at her, dismayed, "Even if that happiness is merely an illusion? Why should we deceive her? To satisfy our egos? Should we become martyrs for her sake? It would be a sin to her... to be deceived by someone she trusts so much!"

"You don't understand," she insisted. "I love her. I need her to smile with happiness. I need to see love in her eyes and gratitude towards God in them... only you can give her that. This illusion will be our last gift to her."

"It's not a gift. It's a mockery of your friendship. You're laughing at her plight," he retorted, his condemnation scathing. Yet, she remained resolute in believing what she was doing was right.

A cruel streak prompted him to challenge, "What about my feelings? Don't they matter? What if I told you I loved her too... once more than life? What will you feel if I hug her close?"

Tampha felt a sharp stab of pain tear at her, "Even then, go to her... go and tell her that! Hug her close and make her feel loved." Tears brimmed in her eyes, shimmering like dewdrops on her lashes before trickling down her cheeks. He exclaimed sharply, reaching out to wipe her tears away. In a hoarse whisper, he apologised, "I'm sorry, I didn't mean to hurt you. It was all in the past. It's you I love now. You know that very well.

He never intended to hurt her, so he continued, "That love held nothing substantial. It was made of mere images and sensations, like a beautiful dream. You are my reality now...!"

She whispered, "But to her, you are very real!" then, with a sudden desperation, she said, "Tell me about her, everything!" She had to know, even if it hurt.

"What is there to tell; she was only a dream!"

He remembered her standing silently among her friends at the hostel night one crisp autumn night. She stood forlorn.

Lost. Entrancingly beautiful. Her innocent beauty and vulnerability caught at his throat and drew him to her inexorably...crowds milled around her in an excited chatter of voices, but she seemed lost in her world. Sensing him watching her, she receded in upon herself, tense and coiled up tightly like a spring. He found himself walking up to her slowly. She watched him fascinated, mouth slightly agape, waiting expectantly for his approach. Yet, at the last moment, as he neared, she turned abruptly and fled. He didn't see her afterwards for the rest of the evening. It had always been like that. There were many such incidents when he had tried ... and she had always run away like a frightened deer at his approach.

The image of her running away from him invaded his dreams, so he tossed and turned with restlessness in his sleep. Her huge, haunted eyes held so much, yet she always turned and hurried away, eluding all his efforts to converse.

Eventually, hurt and bruised, totally bewildered about how to deal with this endless agony and frustration, he stopped trying to reach out to her. Then, she left Chandigarh after her graduation. He had stayed on to complete his internship, after which he went on with his house job. Now, he has his job at RIIMS. Then, after many lonely years, the bright, chirpy nurse, with her vivacious shining personality, had come smiling into his life like a bright ray of sunshine filling up the dark niches and corners of his heart, making his life complete in every way. He wouldn't change it for anything else in the world. Not ever.

♥

Tampha had never been able to rest in peace after Dina had revealed the name of the man she had loved.

"Pradip... he must be a doctor by now!"

Preoccupied with her memories, Dina had failed to notice that her friend had gone deathly pale. Tampha was stunned. Pradip. Her Pradip. Her beloved Pradip. Her fiancée. They were engaged to be wed in a few months: Pradip, the young, earnest, dedicated doctor working in the surgery department of the same hospital. Tampha's heart refused to believe it; it couldn't be true. How could destiny be so heartless, so unforgiving? Yet, the worst was still to unfold. Dina spoke gently,

"It's been years... but I know he loved me, Tampha; he longed for me, just as I longed for him... if he knew of my illness, he would rush to my side. He wouldn't pity me, for he truly loved me. In love, there is no space for pity. There's sorrow, anguish, remorse, but never pity. You might not believe me, Tampha, but he once loved me." She continued, her voice filled with longing,

"If only I could tell him how deeply I love him, I could depart this world content, though it wouldn't be fair to him. He should remain unaware; it is better for him to erase it all from memory."

♥

The haunting reverberations of Dina's story had spread like venomous poison through Tampha's system, consuming her entirely. She became an insomniac, a bundle of nerves – it was a nightmare that sapped her vitality.

The once bright and cheerful Tampha had become a mere shadow of her former self; her vivaciousness and warm smile were lost. The seductive dimples that once graced her cheeks had faded away. She became sad and listless, prompting Dina to inquire anxiously, "Are you sick, Tampha?" to which Tampha could only shake her head and hurry away, muttering,

"'I have work to do, I will be back". It pained Dina to witness her friend's sudden and inexplicable distance. Guilt wracked Tampha, knowing she was causing Dina pain.

Then, one day, the idea struck, and she felt as though a great weight had been lifted from her shoulders. Now she knew what she had to do. She sought out the young doctor, her determination unwavering, her mind made up. "Please go to her. Show her your face. Tell her that you love her," she implored. She felt guilty about betraying her best friend with this grand deception. Still, she convinced herself that when reasoning about love, one must proceed from higher, more important considerations than the popular notions of morality, conscience, truth, or falsehood—or rather, one must not reason at all. She looked at the young doctor pleadingly, "Please do me this favour. Go to her!"

Finally, he relented. "Okay, if that's what you want," he conceded. And so, Doctor Pradip entered the sick girl's room at the hospital that day.

== Endnotes ==

(i) Mother in Meiteilon
(ii) Address to elder brother
(iii) Antakshari, is a kind of singing game played in India. Each contestant sings the first verse of a song (often Classical Hindustani or Bollywood songs) that begins with the consonant of the Hindi alphabet on which the previous contestant's song ended.

7

Nocturnal Hero

In the quiet of the night,
When the night is dark and eerie
Strange things happen,
A somniloquist speaks his dreams,
And a thief searches for his prize.

Amubi had endured the burden for years, the weight of which seemed lesser a few months ago when she was still a vegetable vendor at Ima Market. Now that her son Moba had forced her to retire from the arduous job – which made her so tired but breathed life into her evenings, granting her the sweet surrender to sleep after a day of honest toil – she has started experiencing many a sleepless night. In the quiet of her home, sleep eludes her, and the nights stretch on endlessly. Oh, her poor, poor son! He doesn't even know how he keeps inflicting this insufferable burden upon the frail shoulders of his poor, widowed, and ageing mother.

Moba, her son, always talked in his sleep with a clear, vibrant voice as if conversing with someone else. His annoying habit compounded her insomnia; she tossed and turned in sleepless agony every night, a captive audience to his dream-induced dialogues as he rambled on and on in realistic conversations with imaginary phantoms.

Should she go back to selling vegetables at the Ima Market? She had retired on her son's insistence, but the cessation of her regular activity was not good for her; it gave her insomnia; she was missing the constant din and chatter of the market, the mental stimulation it provided her, leaving a void filled only by restless nights. But Moba was adamant.

"Ima[i] , it's time for you to rest and for me to provide. Why should you sweat in the hot sun from morning till night at your age? You deserve the rest."

"But Ibungo[ii], work suits me. I am used to it!"

The ceaseless bustle at the Ima Market[iii] was her lifeline, warding off the spectre of solitude as she valiantly shouldered the upbringing of her son alone. This whirlwind of activity also played gatekeeper, ensuring that hunger was a transient guest, not a permanent resident in Amubi and Moba's dwelling.

Her tired old bones had protested at night every time she returned from the sweltering marketplace. The domestic duties that awaited her only added to her exhaustion. Surrendering to fatigue, she would collapse into a deep slumber as soon as her head hit the pillow; she had always slept like a log. However, now, granted a respite from her labours, she yearned for the familiar chaos of the market. She was market-sick, missing her work and her companions. The house was too oppressive and quiet when Moba left home for his work. Solitude was an unwelcome companion, so she threw herself fervently into household chores and cleaning, maintaining an impeccable home. Though tired in limb, her thoughts remained sharp and vigilant, piercing the silence well into the night. The time had come for Moba to find a wife, a partner to fill the void of loneliness that lingered like an uninvited guest in their house. Moba's thoughts resonated with his mother's as he spoke,

"Ima, you are always working. Despite your rest from the market, you sweep, cook, scrub, and tend to the vegetables in the kitchen garden. All this work is too much for you. I must find someone... soon..." His voice trailed off, tinged with a hint of shyness.

"Do so, Ibungo. If your heart finds favour with someone, tell me. I'll go and speak on your behalf," she replied.

"But Ima, what if they turn us away? What if they meet your proposal with scorn?" he fretted.

"Let me worry about that. If you're hesitant to approach her, I'll step in. There has to be someone out there for you". Amubi said, the weary lines on her face softening into a smile. Yet, she couldn't help but shake her head sadly as her optimism was at war with the reality of their humble means.

Moba smiled sadly, reminiscing about past misadventures. The scornful laughter of the charming young women he had awkwardly approached at Thabal Chongba[iv] and other local celebrations echoed in his mind, sowing seeds of doubt that any of them would ever regard him as a potential suitor. He was acutely aware of what he lacked: the striking looks, the magnetic charisma, the wealth, a distinguished career, and above all, the self-assurance that seemed to come so naturally to others.

Yet, in recent times, his thoughts had increasingly wandered to Leibaklei—the local belle whose cheeks turned a soft shade of pink and whose lips curved into a shy smile whenever she caught sight of him. She would smile coyly at him, her lengthy hair cascading down her back, as she and her friends gathered water from the expansive pond in front of their sangoi[v]. Her gestures offered gentle encouragement, but Moba had never mustered the courage to bridge the gap between them with words.

In his professional life as an L.I.C[vi] agent, Moba displaced unwavering determination. He dealt with the currency of trust, and he worked tirelessly to earn it from those who considered entrusting him with their life's savings. He was not as smooth in speech and suave in manner as many of his contemporaries who were successful L.I.C agents, yet he wasn't trailing behind in the race for clients. His eyes shone with a sincere light that endeared him to others. His shy nature exuded warmth that made people feel safe and secure with him.

Amubi hoped fervently that someday, a kind-hearted woman would love her son for his priceless qualities. Unfortunately, society often favoured outward trappings and superficial qualities and rarely tried to discover the gems hidden within. And so, Moba remained on the sidelines, whatever interests he evinced in the coy damsels drowned out by laughter at his timid approach and his invisible cloak of self-doubt.

Amubi was the silent witness to her son's romantic misadventures. It wasn't that he poured out his heart to her; instead, he spilled the secrets in his slumber. As she lay awake in the stillness of the night, his whispered words painted a vivid picture of his romantic escapades. Of late, his nocturnal narratives had taken a turn, frequently featuring Leibaklei—a paragon of gentleness and grace whose dignified conduct won Moba's mother's admiration. Amubi liked Leibaklei, with her long tresses, simple clothing, shy demeanour, and respectful manner, unlike the modern lasses with their superior airs and condescending attitude towards older adults of Amubi's generation. She was also a hard worker, crafting exquisite phaneks[vii] on her loom morning till night and earning her income. Amubi imagined Leibaklei at her loom, the rhythmic dance of her hands weaving not just phaneks but, perhaps, unwittingly, the threads of a future with her son.

Amubi's heart swelled with hope and helplessness, wishing upon every star that Leibaklei's heart would sync with the rhythm of her son's dreams. Even the fact that she was from their own Leikai, which could raise eyebrows, seemed a trivial thing to Amubi's matchmaking mind.

The thought of Leibaklei becoming her daughter-in-law brought a smile to Amubi's face, which warred with the furrows of worry that creased her brow. She hoped to introduce Leibaklei to the intricacies of their family traditions, watching her adapt and adopt them with her usual gentle grace. She could teach her the secret recipes passed down through generations, ensuring that Moba always finds the taste of home in every meal.

But for now, Amubi was content to listen, to learn the landscape of her son's heart through his midnight monologues. And as the first light of dawn crept through the window, she would often find herself whispering a silent prayer to the universe – for love to find its way, for Leibaklei to see Moba not just as the boy next door but as the man who could match the steady beat of her industrious heart.

Moba's circumstances were far from ideal, a fact that did little to ease the situation. To describe their living conditions as 'somewhat disadvantaged' would be an understatement.

Their house was old, and the walls cracked and moaned as if having a personal vendetta against them. The roof seemed to have so many holes that sometimes water leaked in during storms. Moba would climb onto the roof and try to repair the house as best as he could. He optimistically, would say that his house was 'ventilated to perfection' much to Ima's chagrin.

Moba dreamed of accumulating enough savings to construct a decent dwelling for his mother. She had dedicated her life to his well-being, with relentless effort ever since the passing of his father. He was just a child of five years when unknown assailants cut short his father's life.

The motive? Lost in the shadows! A legal inquiry? Absent! Justice was not served to the poor woman and her son, and the crime languished unsolved in dusty police ledgers. The death of a humble day labourer was simply not worth the resources of the police. Amubi thus became a widow and a single mother at 33 years of age.

She stood alone, defiant against the negativity that prevailed over a single woman eking out her living alone with a young son. Such women usually fall easy prey to society's degrading forces. Not Amubi. Her quiet dignity and grace formed insurmountable barriers that shielded her from the lecherous advances of predatory men. She thus nurtured her son Mona, who soared academically. Yet, the financial barriers were insurmountable, blocking his path to higher education and a prestigious career. Amubi's coffers were not deep enough to secure the keys to these golden gates.

Moba, however, remained undeterred by the siren call of a less righteous path and the other 'way of life' in a conflict-torn land, either of which had ensnared many of his disillusioned contemporaries. He carved his trail as an L.I.C agent and became increasingly successful.

They live in their run-down hut, which threatened to crumble any day... Their most treasured asset was not gold or jewels but a kinetic Honda, cradled in a makeshift garage - roughly constructed on their mamang[viii] sangoi.

Moba had managed all his life on his travel-worn cycle – And it had been many years that he had been on the cycle – going from home to home on his rounds; he was neither old nor young, in the mid-years between old and young.

But Amubi had insisted, "Ibungo, buy yourself- what do you call it Honda! It would be swifter, speedier; it must tire you out riding from morn till night on your bicycle...!". His mother was right. He needed the vehicle for his endless rounds. But sacrificing some 50,000 from the savings of so many years intended to build up towards a cosy house would be such a pity.

"Ibungo, don't worry about the house; we can manage it in this hut. We have always managed, haven't we?" Amubi had said earlier. Later, she looked intently at her son going towards his mid-thirties and exclaimed,

"You will need to build a better house for your marriage...should we forsake the vehicle...?"

The heavy lines on her forehead became accentuated as Amubi pondered. But hearing the note of concern tinged with worry in his mother's voice and resisting the temptation to give in to the image of sweet Leibaklei coming unbidden to his mind, Moba drew himself up to his full height, expanded his chest broadly, and said proudly,

"Ima the girl who marries me will accept me for what I am, house or no house. We will buy the vehicle first!" That was that. Hence, the Kinetic Honda sat proudly on their sangoi...

♥

Another man walked that eerie moonless night with a different problem on his mind while Moba and Amubi settled down for the night. He needed a fix; soon, the trauma would begin. His supplier agreed to give him a few pinches of the stuff, provided he paid his earlier dues. Now, where would he get the Rs 10,000 he desperately needed?

His earning elder brother and family had barred their door against him. He had no one who cared other than his frail old mother. He was jobless because his family lacked the money and connections to buy a job for him, especially as his father had retired when he was growing up. His father had not been prudent enough to save for his younger son...and while elsewhere, Moba worked hard with his efforts and was going somewhere, he took the path of escapism, drowning his pain and frustration in drugs.

Now, his mind was consumed with a thirst for money- hard, hot cash!

Then the crazy idea came, urging him to do it soon. He must steal- money, property, anything. That was why he walked alone that moonless night, marking his slow steps on the hard tar macadam road, fearing he might run into a police patrol. Every unearthly sound made him jump. A guilty mind is a terrible weight, and he was new to the game.

He was lucky; he saw the rundown house. It was easy to dismantle the gate. But would such a poor-looking house hide anything of value?

"Let's try my luck," he mumbled as he stealthily approached the house. The absence of a dog was a bonus in his favour. He knew he couldn't accomplish his task with a loudly yelping dog lunging at him from the darkness. As he gripped the small knife in his hand, a horrible thought crossed his mind: he could slit the dog's throat. But he loved animals, so he was relieved it didn't happen. After all, he didn't want to awaken the sleepy inhabitants of the house either.

Then, as he was about to try his luck with the house, something caught his eye- the moonlight glinting off the massive lock on the wooden door of the makeshift garage.

"Umm, there must be something of value inside." Gleefully, he approached the shed. He fiddled with the skeleton key he held in his hand in his attempt to force the thick lock, but he lacked expertise. He sweated profusely, and his hair seemed engaged in a perpetual struggle with the clinging sweat as it attempted to stand on end. After what seemed to him to be hours, the lock snapped. Excited, he was about to enter when suddenly he heard the booming voice. The sound floated out through the widely open front window of the house, which was very near to the sangoi.

"Just wait! I have a gun with me; you are dead...." he froze. Someone was awake in the house with a gun. For interminable seconds, he stood still while the voice continued,

"Still waiting? Now you have had it!"

His frozen legs came to life at these words, and he turned and fled, dropping his tools. In his panic, he tripped and fell over some bricks lying near the gate. As he fell, he hit his head against a brick, and blood spurted profusely from the wound. Oblivious to the pain, he pressed his hand against his wound and fled.

Inside, Amubi frowned; her son was at it again. Will he never learn to shut up at night? He was now talking about killing somebody. From where did her gentle son get such violent notions that he had to turn violent in a dream? Amubi wondered as she tiredly tried to stuff her pillow against her ears to drown out her son's voice. Perhaps she had better shift her bed to the kitchen, far from her son's room. But then.... Moba, despite his age, was still a child at heart...so sensitive and easily hurt.

As the morning sun rose on the horizon, casting its golden rays over the town, the usual tranquillity of the house was pierced by the sound of giggling leikai[ix] girls who had come to fetch water from their pond. Leibaklei could be heard giggling and chatting with her friends. The merry peals of her laughter floating on the breeze, sweet like tinkling bells, roused Moba from sleep. How could they enter their yard when the gate had not been opened?

Mother and son hurriedly got up at the same time.

It was Moba, with eyes wide as saucers, who stumbled upon the shattered remains of the lock, the tools of its demise scattered carelessly like breadcrumbs left by a forgetful thief.

"Ima! look! Someone broke this lock", he exclaimed excitedly.

"Oh Iswar Ibungo[x] .... did they...?" Amubi didn't dare specify.

Moba, with great trepidation, peered cautiously inside, "No, Ima"; he heaved a sigh of relief. "It is still inside; wonder why they didn't take it?"

He gazed timidly at Leibaklei, who stood silently with her left arm wrapped around a sanabun[xi], hugging it tighter against her waist – her cheeks aflame with a rosy hue when Moba's gaze lingered on her – waiting while her friends took their turn fetching water from their pond. He remained frozen, his feet rooted to the ground.

Amubi, with a grin spreading across her face, called out, "Girls, our garage lock's been tampered with, and the culprit dashed off hurriedly and even hurt himself. Let us find out why!"

"Oh, Ine[xii], did they swipe anything?" Leibaklei's pals inquired, concern etching their features. "Not a thing," Amubi replied, her voice trailing off as she approached the gate with measured steps. Reaching the gate, her voice rocketed in volume, "Oh my!"

The girls, propelled by curiosity, sprinted to her side. "Ine, what's caught your eye?"

Amubi, with a detective's keenness, gestured towards the chaotic array of bricks stained with telltale crimson—a clear sign the intruder had made a clumsy escape.

Amubi pondered loudly, "Why did the thief make such a clumsy exit without even taking our Honda? Something must have frightened him".

Amubi wracked her brain, seeking a plausible explanation for the thief's inexplicable flight. Suddenly, a lightbulb flickered on. Could it be possible?

"Ibungo, last night you were talking in your sleep about guns and killings. Do you remember that dream? You were almost shouting that you will kill someone......"

Moba scratched his head sheepishly while a merry twinkle lit up his eyes.

"I am drawing a blank, Ima. But last night, my mind was replaying those grim headlines—rival factions clashing... such senseless violence... brother against brother..."

Amubi stared wondrously at her unbelievably conscientious son, but the humour of the situation ultimately got to her,

"Ha! Ha! Ha!" she burst out into merry peals of laughter,

"Maybe the thief thought you were awake and would shoot you and thus ran away...Your talking in your sleep has saved your Honda!"

Leibaklei stared at Moba with an amused smile on her face; her eyes betrayed something more, a longing, a need, while he blushed crimson at his mother's words. New hope sprang in his heart: he would talk to her alone soon, but for now, he blushed as the girls called him 'Sleep-talking Hero'.

== Endnotes ==

(i) Mother
(ii) Address to a younger male, also to son.
(iii) A market at the centre of Imphal town, where women mainly are the sellers.
(iv) Local dance of the Meiteis of Manipur.
(v) An outhouse on the front lawn.
(vi) Life Insurance Company of India, an insurance company based in India.
(vii) Sarong like wrapper which women of Manipur wear.
(viii) Front of the house.
(ix) Locality
(x) Address to God. Iswar means Lord (God)
(xi) A vessel for fetching water, with a small neck a round bottom, and facilitates carrying around the waist by young ladies.
(xii) Aunty

8

Twin Souls

Two parts of one whole,

Linked by an invisible astral cord,

That can never be severed.

Until that day when they will unite,

Both will remain empty, lonely, and incomplete.

Searching each other in every face.

Seeking each other in every voice,

Wandering like lost souls in limbo.

Langlen, once the star pupil of her school, was now the subject of her peers' ridicule. All those who knew her from childhood pitied her, and whispers followed her as she walked the corridors of her workplace. She, who had always been at the top of her class, seemed to have relinquished her zest for life. Her ambitions for career advancement lay dormant, and her choice of a spouse—a man deemed uneducated by societal standards—only fueled the gossip. Yet, Langlen appeared indifferent to the opinions swirling around her.

That day was a holiday; her husband had gone out with his friends as usual. Langlen tried to tidy up her house, which had long been neglected and was now about to receive much-needed care. As she turned the contents of her cupboard upside down, something caught her eye: an old envelope stashed away inside that cupboard.

Langlen's heart almost missed a beat. She whispered, "How have I kept this piece of my past in such a careless manner? Thank God he never looks inside my cupboard!"

It was a letter that she had never sent, dated January 17, 2009.

♥

My twin soul,

I know you felt it at that moment—the feeling that we have been and are one. Words were not required as our souls rushed towards each other in joyful recognition. We were one; we have met and loved before in another lifetime.

Let me tell you about my premonitions and dreams about you even before I knew you. I joined the Association: Women Matters (WOMAT) in June 1996. One magical night around that time, I had a dream. I felt the presence of a man beside me—waves of love emanated from him, filling me with peace and complete well-being. The intensity of emotion amazed me, for I had never experienced such a

feeling. I wrote down the experience in my diary on June 26, 1996.

Langlen paused, then whispered, "Was it just a dream?"

The letter continued describing her fateful decision to enlist the lawyer.

Your name immediately came to mind when our association needed an excellent lawyer in December 1996. It felt as if it was etched into my subconscious. I know it must be because I had read your name in the newspapers about your fight against injustice and advocacy for the just, helpless, and oppressed.

I recommended your name, and we set out to meet you. Though I had always been tongue-tied, words gushed out of my mouth when we met in your chamber. You listened intently, with a slight tilt of your head and an amused smile playing on your lips.

A vivid memory replayed in Langlen's mind: the memory of that meeting.

Langlen's colleague, Thaja, nudged her as they stood outside the lawyer's office. "Nervous?"

"A bit," Langlen replied, clutching her notes tightly.

As they entered, the lawyer stood up and greeted them. "Good afternoon. Please, have a seat."

The instant their eyes met, a feeling of Deja Vu, of instant recognition, assailed Langlen's senses.

"I knew you; I have known you.... not slightly, but intimately..." She felt as if she was replaying a scene from an unknown past.

Langlen's words flowed unexpectedly. "Tamo[i], we desperately need your help. Our association is fighting for fair employment practices against the malpractices that plague our society at present..."

He listened, nodding thoughtfully. "I understand. Tell me more about your case."

Feeling a surge of confidence, Langlen continued. "We believe you are the right person to represent us because of your principled stance and unmatched record."

He smiled slightly. "We'll do our best. Let's work together to ensure justice is served."

♥

Langlen reminisced. "He had such a way of making me feel heard, and I have never been that vocal, " she thought aloud.

♥

Do you ever remember that day we first met? I was in 12th standard in school then. Papa had informed me the day before about your wife's desire to meet him for some work related to a project she was working on. An appointment had been scheduled with Papa.

Early that morning, our dogs, Timmy and Poky's relentless barking disrupted the calm. As I entered and opened the windows of our drawing room and looked out upon the lawn, I looked straight into your eyes, bespectacled, exuding a joyful smile. Clad in a white shirt and black pants, hands tucked in pockets, you stood alongside her—more sensed than observed. I felt something that instant. I remained speechless for what seemed to be an eternity, lost in a whirlwind of thoughts. "How could she snag such a handsome man? Oh, how fortunate she is!" The dark poison of envy had snaked its way into my heart for the first time that day.

I admit I was out of line. When our paths crossed again later, I had forgotten the impact you had on me during our initial meeting. My decision to enlist you as our legal representative stemmed from all the good things I have heard about your reputation. I read how

you have fearlessly challenged corrupt individuals in positions of authority. Your notable cases–particularly those that exposed dishonest practices by public figures or the misuse of power to secure positions for undeserving individuals – struck a deep chord with me.

I admired and respected you and felt that you must be a great human being and a noble soul. These preconceived notions ingrained in my foolish mind affected my instantaneous feelings for you. I trusted you on sight and divulged more than I would do to others, a departure from my usual guarded nature around men.

I thus came to know you through the activities of our association and fell in love with you almost instantaneously.

Langlen remembered the day she became aware of her feelings. It was a day when she had come late to court. She had come rushing in, worried that the proceedings might have started, and she had missed it. Luckily, he was standing chatting with her colleagues.

17 January 1997– Do you remember that day when I came late to court, and you teased me,

"We haven't started the proceedings yet as we were waiting for you; we couldn't start without you. You are the most important member!"

Your words were playful, yet suddenly, it seemed as if a realisation struck you, and I sensed a shift in your demeanour- I felt that your words took on a more profound significance for you. Did you fall in love with me that day the same way that I did?

Langlen remembered how her attention was then drawn to the absent button on his shirt—a detail that captivated her thoughts for the remainder of the day. The charm of that missing button led her to ponder whether his spouse neglected his needs–she had not taken the time to sew the button back in place. Her colleagues had ordered tea, but then he left abruptly without taking his tea. Langlen felt the urge to ensure that he drinks his tea. But what is she to him? Nobody! But why did she care?

That night, without conscious thought, I picked up the diary of 1996, chose an empty page and wrote down my feelings of that day- 17 Jan 1997. I had chosen the empty pages of a diary of 1996 to pen down my feelings of 17 January 1997.

I later discovered that the page I had chosen was that of 27Th Jan 1996, next to the page of 26 Jan 1996, on which I had written down my dream account.

I felt the mystical connection between you and the man of my dreams—the same dream where I sensed a presence beside me, enveloping me with an aura of peace and complete well-being. You were the same. It was you whom I had seen in my dream—even before I met you in real life, other than that one day at home in the distant past.

Note that 26=2+6=8. Also, 17=1+7=8, and 1997 gave 1+9+9+7=26=2+6=8. I am a number 2 person. According to numerology, number 2 persons often have the number 8 appearing in significant life events.

Yes, you were the most important thing to have happened to me. I believed I had met my twin soul, for I felt peace and complete well-being with you, just like in my dream.

Notions of immorality, betrayal—everything faded from my consciousness.... It might sound unbelievable, but I had always harboured a deep disdain for women who pursued married men. I never envisioned falling deeply in love with a married man, let alone becoming one of them.

It was different for us—our circumstances were unique. Various mystical occurrences and spiritual

experiences reinforced this belief in the inevitability of our togetherness. I believed our love was predestined, pre-ordained, fated, and transcended societal norms and notions of morality.

I should have distanced myself, but my certainty that you reciprocated kept me from doing so. I was convinced that I had earned a great man's love. In my circumstances, being enamoured with you was almost inevitable. I was besotted; who wouldn't be in my circumstances?

It wasn't until January 17th that Langlen acknowledged the depth of her feelings for him.

For years, she held onto the illusion that her love for him was genuine, convinced that their union was meant to be.

This perception may have been influenced by the person she was—a product of her upbringing and background. Growing up as a lonely child entangled in the agony stemming from her parents' disparate mindsets yet staying together for appearances, she developed into a reserved, socially awkward individual. She longed for a love that was intense and overwhelming, one that could rescue her from her solitary existence. Subconsciously seeking something or someone to fill the void in her life, she believed she had found what she was seeking when she met him.

We were twin souls, two parts of one whole, linked by an astral cord of mystical energies, unfathomable, undefinable, indestructible, which is a testimony to our predestined Love. As Linda Goodman, famed astrologer, writes, "Twin souls are two people who instantly recognise the other half of themselves behind the eyes of each other. Twin souls will sense immediately that they have been and are one. Almost from their first meeting, their spirits will rush together in joyful recognition, ignoring all bounds of convention and custom, all social rules of behaviour, for they are driven by an inner knowing too overwhelming to be denied. Inexplicably, often without a single word being spoken, they know that only with each other can they both be complete in every way. They hardly need to say the words, 'I love you', for they know that they belong together, if not in their present lifetime (due to karmic complications), then in another lifetime. The forces that created twin souls are indestructible; no man can break the tie between them, and they cannot be separated even through the experience of death. Their meeting is pre-ordained /predestined and has the power to unite humanity in peace and good. During periods of separation due to karmic complications or soul testing in the present lifetime, both persons remain empty, lonely and incomplete, but even during such periods of separation, there is a constant pulsing astral communication between them, for they are supposedly linked by a cord that connects them over the miles. During the weary search for one's twin soul, there will be many side trips and many relationships that appear genuine, then fade into disinterest and boredom."

Yes, our relationship felt that way – as twin souls. From the electrifying jolt of immediate recognition sparked by our first innocently unexpected gaze, a whirlwind of emotions arose, drawing us into a vortex of boundless happiness.

Ours was a strange communion in emotional shorthand. Minute gestures and suppressed words spoke volumes. We completed each other's incomplete sentences. Words were lost in the depths of an ocean abundant with silent heart talk and became redundant.

These were the justifications for the enormity of the pain that would afflict two innocent souls—Your innocent wife and child. I believed that we, as twin soul lovers, could bring peace, well-being, and goodwill to this troubled land. I envisioned us combating corruption together. However, we have been separated due to the inevitable karmic soul testing.

During our legal proceedings, I fell ill and had to travel to Chandigarh for a diagnosis, leaving our case midway. Before departing, I urged our mutual friends to present a parting gift to you. They never informed me that the case was unresolved. Your stricken "Why,

why this? Our case is not over yet!" haunted me. My colleagues stayed silent, mere bystanders to the quiet drama of tormented emotions unfolding before them. I remain puzzled as to why I had behaved thus that day, probably due to my thoughts becoming clouded due to medications. I still fail to understand why my colleagues went along with my 'Farewell Gift' and never said a word to let me know that our case was not over. I wonder if you were ever compensated for representing us, dear Mr. Lawyer.

I don't think so. Did you continue the case without receiving any funds from us? My friends told me nothing while I was in Chandigarh. I was bedridden for six months. Though I had left the case midway, with the memory of your "Why, the case is not over yet?'" haunting every step of my consciousness, I did see the verdict in the newspaper; I have it with me. I just was not a part of the association anymore. I don't know if my association ever paid you for your work. I will never know. For now, it has been dissolved, and I am no longer in touch with any one of the members. I wish I could repay you for everything you've done.

Langlen's thoughts were interrupted by a memory of her husband's abuses. Due to her ill health, she could not do heavy work and hired a maid to help her with the chores.

A day ago, she was feeling unwell and had another bout of diarrhoea. Thank God it was a holiday, and she could lie down and rest. Her maid had left after completing the chores, and she was lying down in bed. He came and started his tirade against her.

"Abe, you are so lazy. Every other woman works: cook, wash clothes, clean rooms, and find time to serve their husbands. What kind of woman are you?"

"I am a woman sick with SLE. At least three people I know have died from this disease. Ask my mother-in-law what a doctor told her about me. I am not supposed to do heavy labour. I have to let money work for me. Anyway, I am not feeling well today".

Her husband jeered, "Not feeling well indeed. Does Madam ever feel well on any day? Yeah, you want to live like a queen. And that man you are talking about must be your lover".

That made Langlen seethe, "Say anything you like, but please do not talk of another man."

"So, you prefer privacy about your lovers?" he mocked as he walked away from her.

Many times, many scenes, endless nagging about her laziness—this was now her life.

♥

Langlen continued reading her unsent letter.

One good thing came of all this. The belief in your love gave me the strength to fight my illness. Bedridden for six months, I still felt your passion.

Love became my focal point. My aspiration. My future. My wealth. I fervently prayed for you, our love, our relationship, and our life together, even when I faced severe illness. Instead of praying for my health, I prayed for you.

I didn't care who pitied me for my grotesque body, ravaged by illness and drugs – your love would see beyond my ugly body to my heart filled with love for you. I even believed that if you heard about my illness, you would become mad with grief and would come to me. I even hallucinated in January 1998 that you had divorced your wife and that you had revealed your intentions of marrying me to my parents.

The drugs, my tortured imagination, and my illness all combined gave me these hallucinations. And in February 1998, I had this amazing dream.

First, there appeared before me a flurry of brightly coloured cards, and the most beautiful of all: a beautiful hand-painted Valentine's card, which screamed with the intensity of secret emotions that brimmed over, in hand-crafted vivid colours of an imagined scene, the love of a lifetime. There were words on top of the card, a garland of words: I could read just the first two words, "My dearest..." (which looked somewhat like the garland below) before my vision shifted to what was below the garland:

It was an exquisite hand-drawn image of us, entwined in a sweet caress. Your generous ears and adored cheeks, red with the purest of passions, your lips, sweet and wide as in life, touching mine ever so softly. ... both of us with our specs, my tumbled hair falling all around.

It was a drawing that could only have been real and in existence—for my imagination, my subconscious mind could never have created that vivid drawing. My mind could never conjure up what it could not make. I cannot paint or bring that image into my mind.

In the next instant, in that dream, I saw a white envelope with words written on it that read,

"HELP ME OJHA[ii] RAJEN"

My father's name was inscribed on that white envelope.

I was jolted awake with my senses reeling, feeling that the dream was accurate- an astral communication between us, a clarion call.

The dream had to be of natural objects in existence, conveyed to me through the sheer strength of our love– that unique astral bond of mystical magnetic energies connecting us that pulse with life and can never be severed.

You had written an appeal for help to my father. You will not know that I write Oja as Oja and never add an extra h to the word; I have never used Ojha; I write Oja. It was not my mind creating that. It had to be of natural objects in existence, conveyed to me via the astral web connecting us. I know you must know how to paint—how I wish to find out, but I never could, whether you could draw—but I felt that you had drawn the card for me during those days.

THAT WAS MY VALENTINE CARD...

I waited for it, but it never came.

But I continued to believe in your love. I waited and hoped and prayed for you.

It was only much later, when my medications were tapered down, that my conscience poked its ugly head. I began thinking that if I loved you, I should stay away from you; I would only be a burden, not worth breaking up your home for.

Now, I realise I wouldn't have succeeded even if I had tried. I underestimated the depth of love you had for your family and overestimated the feelings I sensed in you. I read too much into every little gesture; forgive me for having dared to presume that I could ever dissolve the indissoluble ties that bind you to your family. Forgive me for this past sinful belief.

Fate helped. I was bedridden for six months, and I couldn't get up from bed for months.

Langlen replayed a scene from the past. She was still overloaded with steroids – medications for her illness – when she had rung her closest friend, Tonia, about her feelings,

"Tania, I love Tamo Sashi; I love him. We were meant to be together."

Her friend Tonia drew in her breath sharply, "How could you love that married man? He is married to his college sweetheart; they had been lovers since their school days and loved deeply.......... how could you even think of interfering in their life?"

"I know Tonia, I am being very selfish, but there are many instances in Manipur where a woman becomes the second wife; I understand their plight now—when one feels the way one does, then you cannot run away...our love was meant to be".

Tonia went cold from her end and said in a voice laced with ice. "I am sorry, Langlen, I am busy." She hung up the phone and never rang Langlen again. A friendship ended.

♥

I am such a silly woman who had never been close to a man, who had never known a man's love before, and yet, in those few moments, I felt the love of a lifetime...the love of many lifetimes.

It is difficult to express in a few words the feelings of a lifetime—twelve years' worth of expectations, hopes and thoughts.

You are great. You are meant to be great. You have a lovely, accomplished woman as your wife and a sweet daughter. I ask you to forgive me for having dared to dream of tearing that beautiful family apart.

I know you will not do that. You will not play around. You will not hurt your loving wife and your loved daughter.

For myself, I have lived the past 12 years with the realisation that I will never love another man again the way I loved you. You have spoiled me for any other man. My heart will never be that involved again. My life is in ruins; my career is in disarray, and nothing interests me anymore.

All I wanted from life was to hear your voice and see your face again. I had so much love to give you. So much. You were loved as no other man on earth had ever been loved.

I believed that we were made for each other, that our love was pre-ordained, predetermined, fated, and destined to be. And strangely, I still believe that. And the separation is just karmic soul testing that has torn us asunder and brought you closer to your family. It is as it should be.

Suddenly, Langlen was jolted back to the present by her husband's angry voice. "Why are you reading so late?" he slurred, stumbling towards her. "Come, I want to eat; serve me food and water."Langlen sighed but didn't argue. "Alright, just a moment," she replied softly.

Silently, she served him. He ate noisily, venting his frustrations. "You think you're so much better? Always reading, always dreaming. What good has it ever done?"

After she cleared the utensils, he called her to bed. Langlen lay still and silent, willing herself to bear the pain. Her eyes traced the designs on the mosquito net, her stillness contrasting with the vitality of his movements. Her thoughts drifted back to the letter's final line.

I know we will meet again, if not in this lifetime, then in another. I will wait for that day, living in limbo, soulless and loveless.

Always yours, A woman who loved you very much.

As her husband snored beside her, Langlen whispered, "My body may be his, but my soul belongs to you, my twin soul. We will meet again, perhaps not in this lifetime, but in another. I will wait for you, forever".

== Endnotes ==

(i) Address to Elder guy, or to elder brother.
(ii) Respectful address to a teacher.

9

Paws of Justice

As the old saying goes,
Though the thief is lucky for ten days,
All it takes is one day,
For the owner's turn to come.

It had been nearly a year since her last visit to our home, marking the most extended absence she had ever had. For half a year, I was confined to bed, and though she probably knew, she never once reached out. Unchanged, she was the same as ever. Sweet as honey, words flowed abundantly from Nenei Bino's small, pursed lips. The sheer quantity of sugary phrases spilling from such a tiny orifice was astonishing.

"Oh, the tears I shed when I learned of your sickness! Nene would've been here if not for the calamity the election brought. I've lost upwards of a lakh of rupees. The weight of crushing debts is a heavy crown upon my brow. Only now do I laugh over it, but to dwell on it is to court madness".

A year back, Nene Bino had vied for a seat on the Zila Parishad of Waroo, a village nestled in the southeastern expanse of Manipur. Running as an independent, she suffered a resounding defeat to the Congress nominee, backed by the former Minister of the area. Initially encouraged by the Minister, Nene Bino was abruptly abandoned, leaving her no choice but to continue her campaign alone.

"Oh, but I secured the runner-up position in the election!"

This was Nene Bino's continuous refrain; we could not help but laugh as she turned every life situation into humour.

She had a rare gift: the ability to make people laugh. Her talent for tickling the funny bone was unparalleled; our house echoed with laughter as she joked and fooled around, using her sprightly body as agile as a ten-year-old child's. She was a one-woman show, a veritable female Charles Chaplin.

Her words were honeyed, capable of sending one over the moon or, just as swiftly, cutting them down when their backs were turned. Her chameleon-like demeanour kept me wary; she tried very hard to coat me with sugar syrup, but when her efforts fell flat, her anger was palpable, and I could sense her tearing me into pieces behind my back. Her visits, dictated by her needs in Imphal, always left me with a sense of foreboding. I sensed an insidious poisonous feeling emanating from her, a toxic undercurrent that belied her outward attempts at suppression.

A native of Waroo, Nene inherited her melodious voice from her father, Oja Tomba, a revered Khongjom Parba singer and a close acquaintance of my father. Her vocal talents graced my father's plays, infusing them with a rich repertoire of folk melodies that brought life to the otherwise austere productions.

Nene was an intermittent presence in our home for about five years. Her stays sometimes lasted up to two weeks, whenever business called her to Imphal. But her departures were as abrupt as her arrivals, dictated by her whims rather than our needs. The enigmatic songstress, Nene Bino, was as unpredictable as she was entertaining.

Once, our whole family had a mild fever after a vaccination, which rendered us all helpless. When she saw that all of us were ill, Nene Bino took off like an alarmed bird in flight. She didn't heed all our pleadings to stay on for a few days until one of us got better. With left arms immobilised and with feverishly aching bodies, we had to manage on our own without any help. She was that selfish.

Her selfishness and penny-pinching ways would surface now and then. She wouldn't part with two rupees for our sake, yet she had no qualms about accepting hundreds from us. Indeed, she did. My mother tolerated her, possibly for the amusement she provided. In my mother's eyes, Nene Bino was a harmless, entertaining bachelorette of forty years with a body as supple and flexible as a rubber ball. We would be in stitches watching her imitate others' gestures and quirks.

Nene Bino's thin lips were effusive in their affection for my mother,

"Oh, Inambem[ii], you're truly like a sister to me. This is my home, and I shall wed in this family's grand courtyard."

We harboured hopes of finding her a match, but where to find such a suitor? She wouldn't settle for a simple village fellow; she aspired for someone with a respectable job, ideally from Imphal. Perhaps she had her share of admirers in her younger days, but time had since marched on. The relentless passage of time etched deeper lines into her skin, yet we never ceased our earnest prayers for a suitable husband for her, despite knowing she spoke of us with scorn behind our backs, as was her habit with others. Was it envy?

"Oh, she's narrow-minded but harmless. Let her be," my mother would say, ever the generous soul.

For every kind word Nene Bino uttered about others, she had a trio of criticisms ready. Craving affection, she would disparage those she disliked in our presence, perhaps thinking it would endear her to us as she railed against those, she deemed our adversaries.

I never witnessed her disparaging them when she joined their company; instead, she showered them with her usual so-sweet saccharine words. I cautioned my mother,

"Mama, do not join her in her slanderous talk. She will flip the script against you and make you sound bad in others' eyes."

My mother retorted with annoyance, "What does it matter? My words are meant for their benefit. If she chooses to share them, so be it. It doesn't bother me."

My concern deepened, "But Mama, she has a knack for twisting the truth. You risk being labelled a spiteful gossip monger. This could sour our relationships further."

My mother dismissed my concerns, "You're overthinking it." I pondered, am I overanxious? Was it my imagination, or were the noxious vapours of brewing malice seeping into our home, tainting our once amicable relations with others?

Who were these others? There is Kaka Noren, my father's friend from his play troupe, a clerk at the Office of the Directorate of Census, who often came over and helped us with tiny little things, like getting our gas, paying our bills, etc. Then there is my father's elder brother, Uncle Somen, his family, his wife and my two cousins. They are our neighbours, and our house was separated from their house by a small courtyard. But it was around our young household helper, Leina, that Nene Bino's subtle allure began to weave like a persistent vine.

Our family was a cosy ensemble of four: my parents, myself—affectionately known as Cheche, the elder sister figure by my youngers, but Baby to my parents—and my younger brother Nongyai. Given my prolonged confinement to bed due to an energy-sapping illness, we desperately needed an extra pair of hands. Enter Leina, a delightful young soul from Chairen, who was nothing short of a blessing. She meticulously embraced the lion's share of chores, transforming our abode into a paragon of cleanliness. Her value was immeasurable; her demeanour was sweet and accommodating. Not once did she baulk at my bedridden directives, nor did she ever retort.

Nene Bino and Leina got on well like a house on fire. Hanubi, 'old woman', was Leina's usual address to Nene Bino. Nene Bino didn't seem to mind. Sugary charm fused remarkably well with an impressionable soul. Nene Bino was lifting a significant workload from Leina's shoulders. "Let me do this work, you rest," she often said to Leina. When the shadows of our dimly lighted kitchen unnerved Leina at night, Nene Bino comforted her, assuring her with a lullaby-like soothing voice, "Think of me as your mother. What is there to fear with your mother beside you?"

Over the next few days of Nene Bino's inexplicably prolonged stay, Leina's character transformed. She started answering back when I scolded her for minor mistakes. It was new to her character. This newfound assertiveness grated on my nerves.

One fine day, I chanced upon Nene Bino and Leina whispering conspiratorially; there was an abrupt cessation of conversation when I came upon them. A stammer, a change of topic. The air was thick with the scent of intrigue, and it was deeply unsettling. Dangerous, very dangerous. Co-plotter in some filmy plot?

I voiced my concerns to my mother, "Mama, when will Nene Bino's visit conclude? Her disdain for us is no secret. I suspect she's turning Leina against us."

Mama, weary and resigned, responded, "You're obsessed with her. Let her attempt to sway Leina. Should she succeed and Leina departs, so be it. We're powerless to just let her go. Consider your father's ties to her family."

I'm known for my tenacity in debate, ever eager to advocate my perspective, striving to sway others to my viewpoint. "But Mama," I persisted, "Leina is irreplaceable. Lately, she has become insufferable. It is as if she wants to irritate us so much that we will want her to leave. I don't want her to go away; we need her too much".

My mother scolded me for my rampant imagination. Nene Bino was always so sweet to her, so how could she believe that Bino would poison anyone's mind against us? What would she gain from it? To my mother, it was me with my imagined hurts and grievances that were at fault.

My attempts to sway her with my insights on people—which often turned out accurate—fell on deaf ears.

I was pissed—my oversensitive nerves were stretched taut. The cause: Nene Bino's intimacy with Leina. Is it because I was sick and lonely and stricken with mad jealousy?

That couldn't be the case. Initially, Nene Bino's return after a prolonged absence filled me with joy. Her humour was a balm to the solitude plaguing my convalescence, offering a brief respite from my isolated reality. Yet, presently, every ounce of my being screamed caution. Warning bells rang loud and clear—my intuition. Yet, Mama dismissed my gut feelings as paranoia.

Kaka Noren, papa's friend, was the only one who didn't want to laugh at Nene Bino's joke. He was very rough with her, almost to the point of rudeness. Mama wondered why a naturally mild-mannered person suddenly started to exhibit odd behaviour. She said, "Your uncle Noren seems to have caught your paranoia and bias against Bino. What did you tell him?”

"I didn't tell him anything, Mama".

"You are behaving in the same manner, almost always rude to Bino", Mama insisted.

"Maybe because she deserved it?" I couldn't resist the jibe.

"That's enough. Manners are important, and she is your elder; behave" She looked so sternly at me that I couldn't retort further.

Mama was unfazed even when Nene Bino proved herself a real chameleon. She started to slander Leina, the girl she had professed to care for, like her child.

"Leina has become quite negligent with domestic affairs. Squandering soap, water, everything. And would you believe it? She's secretly eating the milk powder," she accused.

We could only look at one another and wonder whether Leina would do such a thing. We did notice that the milk powder was running out pretty fast.

Mama quipped, "Let's see. I don't believe that Bino. Leina is such a sweet, guileless child."

I thought I saw a note of annoyance on Nene Bino's face, but she controlled her emotion and replied, "As you wish, Inambem, I am just warning you."

Thus, Nene Bino's cunning charm ensnared my family, enchanting us with her wit, inciting frustration with her slander, and occasionally subduing us with her saccharine, sweet words.

♥

One day, the mundane tranquillity of our lives was subtly upended. It wasn't a dramatic upheaval but a delicate tremor of reality peeking through the veil.

The sun beamed down generously, bathing everything in a warm glow. The kitchen was a hive of activity, with everyone, save for my father —who had finished his lunch before us — eagerly descending upon our midday feast. We were all seated around the table: Mama, Nene Bino, Leina, my brother Nongyai, and me. Mother then noticed our cat dashing to the door, a mysterious prize clutched in its mouth.

"What mischief is the cat up to now? What has she got there?" Mother chased the cat and finally grabbed it by the scruff.

"Aha! It is some pieces of fish in a polythene bag! But where did it come from?" Mama wondered.

A round of questioning among the neighbours, who reported no piscine disappearances, led to an inevitable conclusion. With the evidence held aloft for all to see, Mother recounted how she had prepared rou fish the previous evening, storing it in the refrigerator to serve as my daily protein fix.

"It's from our refrigerator, from the rou[iii] I fried last night. But who would wrap it in plastic?"

Breaking the silence, Nene Bino declared, "It belongs to them."

Mother's gaze sharpened, "To whom? Tell us!"

Nene Bino's ears blazed a telltale crimson, yet she offered no words. Her appetite had seemingly vanished that day. She claimed to have dined at her sister's earlier, but perhaps there was another reason for her sudden disinterest in food.

Those fried rou pieces, it seemed, were destined for a journey – they were to be her travel companions as she returned home that evening.

It wasn't a heist worthy of a Hollywood movie or a petty theft that would make the local news. Yet, it was significant enough to shatter our trust in Nene Bino completely. My mother, ever the generous soul, handed her Rs 200 for her journey home despite knowing that Nene Bino had hidden some rou fish pieces in a polythene bag. Once Nene Bino had departed, we conducted a forensic analysis of the refrigerator's contents. A discrepancy in the fish parts matched precisely with the stuff the cat had unearthed from a clandestine nook in the kitchen. Nene Bino had not given due credit to the cat's sensitive nose.

I was liberal with my "I told you so's" regarding Nene Bino's true nature. We had always observed the pattern of vanishing household items—soaps, hairbands, clips, handkerchiefs, and the like—coinciding with Nene Bino's sporadic visits.

Concrete evidence about her duplicity had always eluded us until that day. Nene Bino had not considered the detective cat's sniffing abilities, which ultimately exposed the fishy business. In an act of feline justice, the cat laid bare the truth, leaving no room for doubt in even Leina's mind regarding the whereabouts of those rou pieces.

As the sun set in the evening bathing the horizon in a soft amber glow, we shared the day's amusing tale with Kaka Noren. We carefully omitted Nene Bino's name from the story, but Kaka Noren's intuition was sharp. "This must be about Bino," he deduced, a twinkle of mischief in his eye. "I've meant to tell you something about her, but it wasn't my place to do so."

He leaned in, lowering his voice as if sharing a state secret. "I once saw her stealthily transferring milk powder from your milk jar into a polythene bag. I've been debating whether to inform you, but I didn't want to disturb your relationship. She has also been goading Leina to leave; she asked me once how long she should stay here, that you...." Kaka indicated to me, "You scolded Bino for watching TV always, she told me". He paused, the weight of his withheld confession evident.

I was sharp in replying, "I never scolded Nene Bino ever; I am not that uncouth; she is lying, Kaka."

My mother hushed me up, "Enough, Baby".

Kaka continued, "I know. She is evil. My concern for this family made me so angry with Bino".

This explained his recent behaviour: the absence of laughter at her jokes and the sharp barbs hidden in his comments.

A significant burden was lifted from my mind when Leina's perception of Nene Bino transformed dramatically. She began to see Nene Bino as a deceitful thief. She despised those who would steal, especially from the hands that fed them. With her initial, idealistic views of Nene Bino now in ruins, Leina disclosed every instance of Nene Bino's insidious influence, which had sought to alienate her from our home. She often said, "Girls from Waroo prefer to toil in their own homes and live with honour rather than serve in another's home as if enslaved. Why not follow their example?" Whenever we found fault with Leina, Nene Bino was there, fanning the flames of dissent in Leina's impressionable heart.

Mother was hurt, not by the theft itself, but by Nene Bino's efforts to estrange Leina from us. To poison Leina's mind against us was to wish for her departure. And her departure would mean a relentless burden of household chores for Mother from dawn to dusk. Given her advanced age and frail health, this would undoubtedly take a heavy toll. Nene Bino showed no concern for my mother's well-being.

The sweet, honeyed words were hollow. Mother had even quarrelled with me, defending Nene Bino. Now, it was time for the truth to reveal its face. Nene Bino had taken much from us; in return, she had tried hard to undermine the very essence of our household. It took a cat, guided by some divine intervention, to unveil her true nature. It goes without saying that with Nene Bino's departure, the ambience within our home has dramatically improved.

== **Endnotes** ==

(i) Aunty
(ii) Sister-in-law
(iii) A type of fish

Dark Secrets

I awoke with a start and saw her visage stark,

The red curtains between cast a crimson veil,

Eyes of ember glared at me, hate-filled,

In the trance of night, like a vivid dream.

She hissed and spat at me, chik, chik, chik

I felt the load on my heart, a heavy blow,

And screamed out loud with all my strength.

Nene Bino returned five years after she last left our house, this time with a more ominous purpose. We never desired her return, but the generosity of our own Pabunghan, my father's elder brother, smoothed the way for her comeback. He assisted her in applying for a scholarship in the folk music genre, Khongjom Parva. He even crafted the synopsis for her—a task my equally generous father performed for many other youths. Our father's family had this peculiar knack of wanting to help people, especially Papa and his elder brother. No, they are not doing it for monetary return, gain, or reciprocity. They just loved helping people.

Nene Bino's father, Oja Tomba, was a highly respected practitioner of this distinctive folk art from Manipur. Upon his passing, the expectation fell on his daughter to continue his legacy. Thus, Nene Bino visited our home once more and applied for the scholarship with Pabunghan's help. Out of respect for her distinguished father, my parents overlooked her past theft and malicious gossip transgressions, offering her sanctuary in our house. The subject of Khongjom Parva was novel to the scholarship's sponsors, and Nene Bino's application was accepted.

Her visits were sporadic, lasting 10 to 15 days, during which Pabunghan dedicated himself to writing her reports. It soon became apparent that she had no genuine interest in the scholarship's work and was motivated solely by the stipend of Rs 3000 per month. She never thought of doing something for Pabunghan for his labour and effort. She was free riding. She didn't even spend money while sending the reports, for it was always my obliging, generous papa who saw to it that Pabunghan's handwritten notes were typed painstakingly by his friend Kaka Noren and promptly dispatched via speed post to their destination. She even made me spend money and effort once to complete this thankless task for her.

My temper brewed and fermented when I heard her pour 'sweet nothings' from her mouth. I always feared leaving her alone in the house, remembering her thieving nature, but we were pretty helpless. Mama was, as usual, unperturbed.

"How much can she take anyway? Let her take as much as she wants; it can't deplete our resources."

Her casual manner perturbed me at times. But what can she do about it? Human courtesy demands that we put up with her for those few days. But it was Papa who had grand plans for her. He allowed her to sing and perform in front of an audience. Papa had to stage a play and some programmes for his mentor, Amit Sinha, who was responsible for funding and creating my father's forum for theatre in Manipur. She performed pretty well; her photographs were taken...and enclosed and sent in with her reports. I had to surrender my stand against her. In any case, she was helpful in the home, lifting a load off Mama's back. Not that it compensates for her continuous attempts at disrupting our relationship with everyone else. She was, as usual, poison inside. Then something happened during the course of her stay!

I was usually terrified of the dark. After dinner, it was particularly unsettling for me, with Mama and my youngest sister engrossed in the television in the living room, Papa fast asleep on his bed, and Nene Bino absorbed in the small TV a floor below my bedroom, refusing to retire until late, leaving me to climb to our room upstairs all alone.

Fear always crawled underneath my skin as if it had a soul. My worries had grown lately, though I never did understand why. It wasn't easy trying to sleep. I had to carefully put down the mosquito net and cover my head with a small shawl. Sometimes, with two tube lights on, I lit a candle and desperately tried to concentrate on Ruskin Bond's collection of short stories, 'Collected Fiction.'

I was always a light sleeper, sensitive to sound and movement. Something woke me up that night. Nene Bino was fiddling around at the foot of my bed, evidently searching for something in her bag, with torchlight in her hand. She evaded my question about what she was doing in the middle of the night at the foot of my bed. I repeated my question when she lay down to sleep later. She said she was searching for a Vicks as she had a sore throat. I soon drifted off to sleep.

I was jolted out of my sleep. Then I saw her. The thin red bed curtains between us. My red curtain and hers- light pink...and beyond she was stretched out on the bed, reclining sideways...in her usual attire, a white shirt with tiny pink flowers sprinkled over it, and a red phanek[i]. Her hair fell over her shoulders, all curls. The thin film of redness of the curtains between us shadowed her whole body...making her face redder than usual. But those eyes – blazing red like fiery orbs, flashing an indescribable expression – made my flesh crawl, and goose pimples broke out all over my clammy skin. Before I could compose myself to gather my wits and ask her why she was glaring at me so, she had drawn back her lips – all her teeth showing the way Dracula's women did in the Dracula movie at their unfortunate women – and as in a trance, I stared; in the background, I heard a slow chanting...chik, chik, chik. My heart jolted with heavy, numb pain, and I closed my eyes while my soul screamed with silent agony. I opened my eyes....and that frightening image had disappeared. I could only see an eerie glow in our room from the lantern at our lainingthou[ii] in our parent's room below, reflected from our window ventilator, which was directly above their room. There was the same red film on our two curtains. I couldn't see her sleeping on her bed adjoining mine. The two curtains didn't allow us to see each other. So, what was it that I saw? Was it a dream? It was still so vivid in my mind. So real. What one sees with one's mind differs significantly from what one sees in reality. It was too real to be a dream, but it had to be a dream. I saw a thin white line stretching down my curtain. It wasn't there in that dream image. Or was it? Was it real? Or was it a dream? Had she opened her curtains...and dropped it later? Had I seen her spirit in a dream-like reality? But why should I see her like this? My mind debated as I tried to calm my heartbeat, which throbbed erratically. Composing myself, I called out softly,

"Nene Bino".

She answered, "Um".

I didn't talk about what I had just seen. I just said, "I couldn't sleep". She answered, "I couldn't sleep either!"

I don't know how I fell asleep again that night. But I did. The following day, I told her,

"I saw you in a reality-like dream state glaring and hissing at me at night, and I had a nightmare. Did you use some black magic or something?" There it is, out again, bluntly, from my mouth, that trait that people hate about me so much. She answered.

"I didn't do anything of that sort. I don't know any black magic" She managed to look affronted and hurt as she said these words, but I was not fooled. I knew that she was up to something.

♥

That was not the only incident where she haunted my dreams. It happened again a few days later.

I am a late starter, always the last one to get up. Nene Bino usually got up at around 4.30 am or 5 am. And sometimes, I used to hear her getting up, but I would promptly go back to sleep. Lately, she had managed to get up surreptitiously without making the slightest sound, supposedly so as not to wake me, as I was a light sleeper. Noiselessly, she glided down our wooden stairs, which usually creaked and groaned, even if it was just our cat going down the stairs.

That morning, a few days after the earlier incident, I woke again with a start. I laid eyes on something which made my heart miss a beat. Nene Bino's face was pressed against my bed curtains. I could see it as an outline. Her curly, frizzled, unruly hair spread out. Her nose, lips...temple...the hollow of her eyes...a black smudged outline...and I distinctly heard her chanting a mantra in her voice, unmistakable.

The thought came unbidden into my mind. "So, you have been doing something all along to me". But before I could do anything, she blew her breath at me...whoooooooooooooohhhh. I felt a stab of pain in my heart as if I was going to have a heart attack. I screamed out loud. The next instant...the outline had disappeared. But Nene Bino was coming in from outside– she had been outside the door, not standing beside my bed – and she was too far away to have run outside and come in again at my scream, which was vocal this time. It was another nightmare, a reality-like nightmare again. I could see a faint smile playing on her lips as she asked me,

"Why did you shout?"

"I had a nightmare, but what were you doing now?" She had a ready answer,

"I had just gotten up; I was outside, praying to Surya Deva (the Sun God)."

I told Mama about my dreams; she dismissed them as mere nightmares caused by my fears and compounded by my imaginative mind. I was persistent in my belief.

"Mama, I am sure she is doing something. Didn't you say her father knew black magic? You told me that he and another rival blew spells at each other, and he made the rival's wife, who had recently given birth a few days ago, come running to his side, leaving her newborn baby, right Mama?"

"Might be an old wife's tale, Baby, just rumours...don't overthink it" Mama tried to soothe me, but I was not convinced. I put a cloth curtain between our two beds in case I woke up and saw her peering at me. I was petrified, and even seeing her natural face at night gave me goose pimples.

Nene Bino fell in love. Khemchand, a martial arts expert, often visited Papa. She blushed and stammered when he came and went out of her way to please him, serving him tea with effusive charm and red-stained cheeks. We knew that she had got it bad – the bug of lovesickness.

One particular day, as I wandered into the kitchen, I caught Nene Bino adding a mysterious powder to Khemchand's tea. Curiosity piqued, I inquired, "What are you adding, Nene?" She assured me it was just sugar, but the fine texture of her powder simply did not match the coarse grains of the unopened sugar jar. She insisted that it was sugar; I, for one, suspicious as always, could not believe it.

I recalled how Nene Bino had recently served my tea in a distinct cup. On one occasion, when she handed me a cup brimming with tea, I suggested sharing some with her, only to witness her panic-stricken reaction. She hastily excused herself to fetch another cup, clearly unsettled by the thought of mixing our beverages. This peculiar behaviour planted a seed of suspicion, and I resolved never to accept a cup of tea from her again.

Our culture believes in 'semjanba,' a form of enchantment where certain herbs– prepared by black art practitioners, using mantras and chants–can bend a person to their will when mixed into food and eaten by the victim. Could it be that Nene Bino was resorting to such mystical practices? Was she attempting to influence my actions through her herbal concoctions and perhaps even to ensnare Khemchand's affections with a different blend? The thought lingered in my mind.

♥

It was slightly drizzling that day. Nene Bino was going home that day to Waroo. She suddenly wanted to visit her younger sister, Sheena, who lived at Tera. So, she went on our cycle and borrowed our umbrella, driving with just one hand. It was a lazy Sunday when I didn't have to go anywhere and could be a couch potato in front of the TV. Nene Bino had gone just a few minutes when Mama called me out,

"Baby, hurry, come see this."

"What is it, Mama?" I was curious.

"Bino has left her bag near the front door; it must be while she was unfolding the umbrella that she must have forgotten her bag."

Curiosity overcame me, and I implored my mother, "Mama, can we peek inside her bag? She clings to it all day".

My ever-trusting Mama hesitated, "It is wrong to touch someone's stuff...Only a thief will do that..."

"Please, Mama?" I pleaded.

Mama relented, and we peered inside her handbag.

The first thing we saw was a small, bulky cloth bag. We brought it out. Inside were small satchels containing some white powder that looked like salt. We realised that these must be the powders that she was mixing in my tea, and in poor Khemchand's tea. Our worst suspicions appeared to be materialising: Nene Bino was dabbling in black art. Drinking the tea thus tainted must have induced in me nightmarish visions of her transformed into an evil witch, her eyes glowing crimson with animosity. This substance's impact on Khemchand remained unknown, probably to enchant him and tie him to her irrevocably.

Despite our fear, we delved further into the depths of the bag.

Then we saw a tiny piece of paper, carefully rolled up and bound with a small thread. We unravelled the thread hurriedly, and all the while, our hearts were thudding; we were scared that Nene Bino would return for the bag. As the proverb says: a guilty conscience can be a heavy burden to bear.

On the paper, the following words blazed like a red flame:

"Around your neck, I have tied this noose, like binding a bull with a lasso; you must do my bidding; as I drag you along the floor, you will have no will other than to do my bidding. You are now my slave, and I am your master; your mind is mine to command".

Then some archaic words:

"Om kling klang hum,

Oona mina yaana till,

Ee u o ei, mana ona, sana

Pham bam kang som

....

Chik Chik Chik"

The last words struck me like a thunderbolt; I dropped the paper as if it burnt my fingertips.

Blazing at me were the words I heard in that eerie reality-like dream I had experienced, where Nene Bino glared at me with her red eyes and lips drawn back.

"Oh, what shall we do, Mama? I was right; she had been doing voodoo black magic all along...she must have been chanting this mantra while I was asleep, thus giving me nightmares....!"

Mama's face had gone pale as she pondered our options.

"I think we should throw the paper down the toilet; it is said that doing so destroys its power!"

"But Mama, if she finds out that the paper is missing, she will know that we have taken it out; what if she uses stronger magic against us?" I was terrified of the possibilities.

"You are right; let us put the paper back where it belongs, in her bag; we will let her go and never let her return here again". Mama decided.

"Hurry, Mama, she might come back". As guilty as thieves, we hurriedly picked up the paper and returned it to Nene Bino's bulky bag and put it inside her handbag.

When Nene came back, I was too terrified to talk to her. Mama calmly gave her the bag. "Here, Bino, you had left the bag on the mangol[iii] today.... come, it's getting late; you are late for Waroo". Nene's face turned deep red. She almost grabbed the bag from Mama and looked through the contents. Everything seemed fine; Mama gave her the fare for the trip home.

A few days later, Papa sent word to Nene Bino's family that our astrologer had forbidden people from the South from entering the threshold of our house again; otherwise, lousy misfortune would visit our home.

It became clear that she had recited these words over me as I slept, and it worked its enchantment, giving me those vivid nightmares. Whatever spectre it had called from the grave haunted me in my dreams as she chanted those words. One eyewitness to her activity, who, because of being new to the household, had not dared to inform us, was Bimol, our new driver. He recounted a chilling scene: her silhouette on the veranda outside my room, bathed in the soft luminescence of the overhead bulb, as the clock heralded midnight. There she stood, engrossed in a piece of paper. He had remained silent, wary of his place as the newcomer amidst our longstanding relationship with Nene Bino.

Her sorcery had not succeeded with Khemchand either. He left India and relocated to the US within a few months of the incident.

♥

For years, I suffered from these sleep paralysis-like dreams, and after pujas and all, it stopped for a year or so.... only to come back again.

Scientists and doctors would call it sleep paralysis; our body would go rigid while the nightmare sapped our energy. Many times, it happened. Once, I saw this black thing lying on top of me at night. I, recently attending reiki classes, tried to make reiki symbols with my hands. I was in a dream, in that life-like dream, and I had awareness enough to make the reiki symbol with my fingers. The thing lifted its black hands and moved its fingers, imitating my action. I shouted out the name of my beloved Goddess, help me, Ima Panthoibi[iv] , and I woke up...

On another occasion, I felt something like a swirling energy roving freely over my body, slowly descending. I was not fully awake, caught in that twilight zone between sleep and wakefulness, rendering me helpless to shout or scream. As that swirling energy crossed my navel, I sensed someone entering the room. It was our new young maid, Abe (Leina had left a few years after the incident with Bino; her mother had fallen sick and needed her help at home). Abe opened my almirah to retrieve something. Instantly, the hand ceased its wandering, and I woke up.

Abe called out, "Aunty, good morning. There is no milk in the kitchen, so I have come to take some from your almirah."

"It's okay, Abe. Take it," I said, still shivering with the memory of that dreadful dream.

Sometimes, the entity behaved like a man; sometimes, it was black and shapeless, and sometimes, it took Nene Bino's form, leaving me screaming to the heavens. Visits to priests, traditional priestesses (maibis), and numerous pujas and rituals did nothing to dispel those nightmares.

The nightmares continued until I got new help recently. Ten years after the Nene Bino left our household forever. Her name was Pramo. She did all the work as if it was her own home. I got very fond of her after missing Abe a lot, who had recently married her boyfriend and left my home.

A month after she came, as is my wont, I told Pramo about Nene Bino and her sorcery practice, which still affects me every night.

"Bino. Where is she from?" She asked.

"She is from Waroo village". I told her.

"Oh, I know a Bino from there". Pramo said enthusiastically.

"What is her father's name?" My heart was beating in anticipation.

"Oja Tomba..." Pramo confirmed my suspicion.

"Yes, she is the one," I admitted, saying that the Bino she knew and the one who hexed us were one and the same.

"Oh, then I know her; we were like family friends until an unfortunate incident happened, and we parted ways. I still have her number". Pramo told me about the unfortunate incident through which they parted ways as family friends.

"Oh, do give me that number." I insisted.

She gave me the number, and I rang.

My heart pounded with strange trepidation when she picked up. "Nene Bino?" I asked.

"Who is this?" Her voice was expectant as if some good news was coming her way, good news indeed.

"Baby from Moirang Leirak, do you remember me, Nene?" I sneered. At least I felt that way: like I was sneering at her.

"Oh baby, how are you?" A sugary, syrupy voice answered.

"I am fine now, Nene, but do you remember what you did to me." I was ready to blow.

"What did I do to you?" Sugar syrup asked hesitantly.

"You had this piece of paper where every night and early morning every day, you chanted something about subjugating me to your will, and we found the paper. I had nightmares every time you chanted from that paper. The last line on that paper was 'chik chik chik'. I didn't tell you at that time because we were so scared of your sorcery. We put that paper in your bag." I shoot rapidly like a machine gun firing.

Nene Bino was so stunned that she just gaped at the phone, "You put the paper where?" (She couldn't even say something like "What paper?" to depict her innocence). Her words revealed her guilt. I could now laugh at it.

"In your bag."

"No, no, I never did such a thing."

"You did hingchabi(witch); I now return that spell to you, hanjallo, hajallo, hanjallo(May it return to you). That ghost has been returned to you now". I said and hung up.

I felt a heavy load lifted from my chest, and a profound sense of relief washed over me as I hung up the phone that day. The nightmares ceased, and peace returned to my nights.

I owe Pramo for that.

(i) Wrapper cloth worn below the waist by women in Manipur.
(ii) God of home and hearth.
(iii) Front verandah of the house
(iv) In the Meitei religion of ancient Manipur, also known as Sanamahism, Panthoibi is a goddess associated with many things, including courage, fertility, handicraft, love, victory, etc.

Disclaimer

This book is a work of fiction. Names, characters, places, and incidents are the products of the author's imagination or are used fictitiously.

Any resemblance to actual persons, living or dead, events, or locales is entirely coincidental. The characters and events portrayed in this book are purely fictional and do not represent any real individuals or events.

The author has taken creative liberties in crafting the story, and any similarities to real people, places, or occurrences are unintended and purely coincidental.

The views and opinions expressed by the characters do not reflect those of the author or any entities the author is affiliated with. This work is intended for entertainment purposes only.

About the Author

Sophia Chanu, a teacher in Manipur, finds her true passion in writing stories. With a keen sensitivity and a deep observance of the world around her, she draws inspiration from the myriad experiences and insights she gathers in her daily life. Her stories, though rooted in real-life observations, are unique creations that reflect her imaginative spirit. Her first book is a collection of short stories primarily centred around the theme of love. It explores various facets of romance, from crushes, infatuations, to deep commitment and meaningful relationships.

This debut book marks the beginning of her literary journey, and she aspires to craft even more engaging and entertaining stories in the future.

May I ask you a favor?

At the outset, I want to give you a big thanks for reading this book. You could have chosen any other book, but you took mine, and I appreciate this. I hope you have at least a few actionable insights that will positively impact your daily life.

Can I ask for 30 seconds more of your time?

I'd love it if you could leave a review of the book. That will help me grow my readership by encouraging folks to take a chance on my books.

Keeping it straight - reviews are the lifeblood of any author.

It will take less than a minute of your time but will tremendously help me reach out to more people. Kindly provide your review at the store you bought this book from. And I'd love to see your review. Thanks for your support.